THIRD TIME IS A CHARM

A WITCHES THREE COZY MYSTERY

CATE MARTIN

Cover design by Shezaad Sudar.

Cover images by Aarows via Dreamstime.com.

Ratatoskr Press logo by Aidan Vincent Kise.

ISBN 978-1-946552-90-7

❦ Created with Vellum

CHAPTER 1

*J*ust between you and me, I actually like winter. It's my favorite season of the year.

I know, it's not popular to say that. And don't say it's because I used to play hockey. The hockey I had played was all indoors. It didn't matter what the weather was like outside. I skated when it was over ninety degrees outside, and I skated when it was thirty below zero. Inside the rink, it was all the same.

But for me, there was nothing better than coming out of the locker room after an afternoon on the climate-controlled ice into a world filled with gently falling snow. The way it brushed against my cold-chapped cheeks was like a fairy's kiss.

But when it's just the cold and the wind and no snow? I admit even I find it less than thrilling. And that's what we had had lately, cold wind and no snow. I probably shouldn't complain too much. It is more than a week away from Thanksgiving and far too early in the year for snow, but still.

Who wants cold and wind but no snow?

It was too cold for us to meditate in the backyard together like before. The cellar was warmer, what with the wood-burning stove and all, but getting to the cellar involved first going out into the yard. It didn't seem worth the effort getting into and out of coats and hats and gloves.

So I mostly stayed inside the house. Which was strangely isolating. I mean, Sophie and Brianna were always there with me, but without a larger space, we never gathered together for more than meals. And Mr. Trevor, well, I very rarely saw Mr. Trevor. He was around, but in that invisible way of his, keeping the house tidy and the kitchen stocked with food without ever quite being seen beyond the occasional meal he shared with us.

I was lonely. But I was also a bit frustrated. I was supposed to be learning magic, but that never seemed to be happening.

"There must be a place we can work together," I said in one of the few moments when Sophie, Brianna and I were all in the kitchen at once. I had been frosting the batch of pumpkin pie cupcakes I had made to bring to Nick's grandfather when, by some miracle, both of the other two witches had come in for tea at the same moment. "The library?" I offered.

"No," Brianna said. "I don't want to risk an unstable spell upending things. I have a specific arrangement that can't be disturbed."

As far as I'd ever seen, her specific arrangement was to open every book at once and spread them out over every table, overlapping book on book, occasionally topped by a cup and saucer long since drained of tea.

"I'm with Amanda on this one," Sophie said. "You did promise you'd show us some spells to do with our wands. I want to learn how to do that lightning thing."

"That's a rather advanced spell," Brianna said.

"So show us something we can start with," Sophie said.

"The attic," I said. "Sophie, you dance up there. There's lots of open space."

"Isn't it cold up there?" Brianna asked, a worried line forming between her brows.

"Hey, if a Louisiana girl can take it," Sophie said.

"All right," Brianna conceded. "I was taking a break, anyway. I can spare a minute. But it really has to be just a minute."

We trooped up the stairs together. The attic was indeed cold, probably because there were no heat vents. Some heat did rise up through the floor from the lower levels, but it wasn't much. I zipped my hoodie up a little higher, watching the clouds of frost forming in front of my face with each breath.

"Oh, it's colder than I thought," Brianna said, frowning.

"No worries," Sophie said. She raised her arms in a dancer's pose, drawing herself up on her tiptoes. Then she started to spin around, and I could see swirls of air forming after the motion of her sweeping arms. But it couldn't be air I was seeing. Was it the magic?

Then I felt it; a warm breeze cascading over my body. It blew away the frost of my breath. It filled my nose with the smell of jasmine, with just a hint of fresh roasted coffee and... was that the smell of fresh baked croissants?

My mouth started to water. Those croissants smelled good. I'd put off eating lunch and had refrained from sampling the cupcake batter, as I was planning on having an early dinner at Nick's apartment later, but my stomach only lived in the moment. And in the moment, I would kill for one of those croissants.

"Ooh," Brianna said, turning her face into the warmth of Sophie's breeze. "That feels nice."

"Thanks," Sophie said. "Of course, it's just my usual wandless form of magic."

"Right," Brianna said, taking the hint. She pulled out her wand. It was a narrow slip of wood—I'm not sure what kind—polished until it glowed as if made of gold. It flashed in the air when she waved it about. It rather reminded me of an orchestra conductor's baton.

"Okay, this is a pretty simple spell," Brianna said. I looked over at Sophie, and she rolled her eyes ever so slightly. I gave her a smile. Everything that Brianna said was simple always turned out far more complicated than expected.

"You already know how to focus and channel your energy through the wand," Brianna said, starting to walk in a circle that I was sure was deliberately facing into Sophie's wind. It blew the hair back from her face like she was in a music video. "You're going to imagine something inside your mind. Then you and the wand together will project it as an illusion. It has no physical reality, being just light, so it's a fairly simple thing to get the wand to channel for you. The more you work on it, the more intricate your illusions will become. But you'll also form more intricate connections between you and your wand. So when you need to actually manifest something real, it will come more easily to you. It's a good thing to practice as often as you can. Try to make a lot of different shapes and patterns."

Then she stopped walking, standing in the center of Sophie's swirling breezes. She closed her eyes, then raised her wand up into the air. Not like an orchestra conductor. More like the pose on the poster for Hamilton. She stayed that way for a long moment; then she started stirring the very end of her wand in tiny circles. The circles expanded, bigger and bigger, and I realized that she was creating something with the circles. Each full rotation created a brass wheel that floated up and away as the next started to form. The small ones spread wide under the peaked attic roof, but when the larger wheels formed, they filled in the spaces between.

Then I realized they weren't wheels. They were gears, their outer edges a series of fine teeth that interlocked when they came into contact with each other. And as soon as they were interlocked, they started turning, big ones and small ones together, turning ever faster as more and more wheels joined in.

Soon, being inside the attic was like being inside the belly of some enormously complex clockwork, glinting in the light as the gears rotated, meeting each other at all sorts of odd angles but never locking up.

"Wow," Sophie said, barely more than a breath.

I couldn't say anything at all. I don't think I could even imagine such a thing, let alone create it.

At last Brianna opened her eyes, looked around, and gave a little nod as if it just met her standards.

That she waved her wand again, and the entire thing disappeared. "Who's next?" she asked briskly.

I averted my eyes. Sophie sighed deeply, then took out her own wand. Hers was more roughly shaped than Brianna's, with little knobs on the sides that spoke of daughter branches long since stripped away. I'm not sure what wood she had used either, but she had stained it a deep dark color, a rich brown that was nearly black.

She ran her fingertips over it softly, then held it up in the air. She took a deep breath, then closed her eyes. I could see her focusing on her breath, going deeper into a standing meditation.

The breeze kept circulating around us, and my stomach kept growling. I tried to focus on the jasmine scent. It really was quite lovely, as if from flowers that had just bloomed.

Eyes still closed, Sophie began to move. She didn't spin or dance, just shifted her weight from side to side with her feet still on the floor, but it was very dance-like. Her arms moved in long sweeps, and her wand formed the very tail of that motion.

I saw something on the very tip of her wand, at first just a blob of white. Then it started trailing off the end of her wand as if it got caught in the breeze. As it spooled out, I saw it was a long ribbon of silk, a brilliant snow-white ribbon.

Sophie gave her wand a tight little spin, and the ribbon broke away to dance off on its own, floating on the breeze around the room.

She made another silk ribbon, this one the bright yellow of buttercups. That too danced away across the room, moving faster as if trying to catch up with the other ribbon. She did this a few more times, until a rainbow of ribbons were all dancing around the room, spinning and twisting around each other, whirling around in delicate loop-the-loops.

Sophie lowered her arms to the ground and opened her eyes. The sight of the ribbons dancing around seemed to catch her by surprise, and a delighted smile spread over her face.

"Wow," Sophie said. "I didn't think that would really work."

Brianna clapped her hands. "It's just lovely," she said. "Look at them; they're still dancing."

Sophie reached out to touch one, and it disintegrated just in front of her fingertips, raining down to the ground in a thousand silky droplets.

"Aw," she said. "It looked so smooth; I wanted to touch it."

"Well, remember," Brianna said in a very teacherly voice, "this is just an illusion. We're not yet working on creating tangible things out of nothing."

"When are we gonna work on creating things out of nothing?" Sophie asked, still grinning widely.

"One thing at a time," Brianna said, then turned her attention to me.

I looked down at the wand in my hands. I knew what wood this was. It came from a willow tree. I had cut the branch from the tree myself. My hands had stripped off all the bark and smoothed the wood, had rubbed layer after layer of stains and salves into it, some mundane but many magical. I had done a thousand other things that were supposed to help me bond with this little piece of wood.

And I knew it had worked. The wand had saved my life. In that other place where I could see the webs connecting all things, I had seen that the wand was part of me.

But I wasn't in that place just now. And the wand felt very distinct from me.

"Go ahead and try, Amanda," Brianna said.

"Yes, give it a try," Sophie said. "What's the worst that could happen?"

"*Nothing* could happen," I said. But I closed my eyes, feeling the wand in my hand, not just through my fingertips, but also sensing its presence with my mind.

So far, so good.

I didn't know what illusion I should try to make. It made sense that Brianna would create something of intricate complexity. I was pretty sure she was just showing us the routine workings of her own mind.

And it made sense that Sophie had created something beautiful and dancing. That was the essence of who she was.

But what about me? How was I supposed to sum my own self up?

I guess I didn't want to try. I didn't want to make anything that complicated. I just wanted to make *something*. A little spark of light. That would be enough.

I concentrated, seeing sparks of light in my mind, something like fireworks but smaller. I pictured them as hard as I could, squeezing my eyes tightly shut. I focused on the feel of the wand in my hand, imagining the light flowing from me into the wand. Then I raised my arm, holding it up like the Statue of Liberty holding her torch.

That would be me. I would be the Statue of Liberty.

I couldn't hear Sophie or Brianna. If I was doing anything, if they could see it, they weren't giving me any indication. No feedback at all.

At last, I just had to open my eyes and see for myself.

It wasn't much. Something was coming out of the end my wand, something like a little bit of a spark, but it was more like dull embers than fireworks, and they just fell out of the end of it, turning to bits of ash before disappearing entirely when they hit the floor.

"Well," I said. I could think of nothing more to say.

"It was a good start," Brianna said. "Please don't get discouraged."

"No, of course not," I said.

"Why don't you try again?" Sophie said.

I looked down at the wand in my hand. I strongly suspected I would get better results without an audience, even though Brianna and Sophie were both being super supportive. I wanted more practice, but I wanted to do it alone.

"Not right now," I said. "Brianna probably wants to get back to whatever she's working on, and I should really start getting dressed."

"Wearing something special?" Sophie asked in a teasing voice. "Trying to impress grandpa?"

"Don't be silly," I said, feeling my cheeks heat up. "It's not that big of a deal."

"Meeting his family is always a big step," Sophie said. She looked to Brianna to back her up, but Brianna just looked confused.

"What's going on?" she asked.

"Amanda's date night," Sophie said, giving Brianna a playful nudge with her elbow. "Keep up."

"It's not a date," I said. "It's just dinner with his grandfather. I guess he's worried that Nick isn't socializing enough since coming home from Afghanistan. I'm just there as proof Nick's not becoming a recluse."

"That, or you're just not calling it a date because you're keeping your options open between two time periods," Sophie said with an arch to one eyebrow.

Poor Brianna looked more confused than ever. "What do you mean?"

"I mean Edward," Sophie stage-whispered.

"Oh," Brianna said. I would swear she was exaggerating her sudden understanding for effect if I didn't know for a fact that Brianna never dabbled in sarcasm. The look she fixed on me was dead serious. "Edward is nice, but I think you should confine your dating to people living in the present."

"I'm not dating anyone," I insisted. "Honestly, I have enough on my plate mastering this magic thing. I don't need more complications in my life."

"And yet," Sophie said, "life always makes more complications."

"Not if I can help it," I said, tucking my wand away. "It's just a dinner with an old man who's worried about his grandson. It's a favor for a friend. That's it."

"I didn't mean to upset you," Sophie said, and I took a deep breath.

"I'm not upset," I said, although that was half a lie. But there was a wistful look in Sophie's eyes, and I remembered that, unlike me, she had had a life that she had left behind to come to Miss Zenobia Weekes' School for Exceptional Young Ladies. A life that had included someone she was close to.

"I'm not upset," I said again, and this time I *did* mean it. "But I am going to be late. Brianna, I'm totally going to practice more on my own later."

"Let me know how that goes," Brianna said, but her voice had that faraway quality that told me she was already thinking about whatever she was about to return to in the library.

"And have fun on your not-a-date," Sophie added.

"I will," I promised, then ran down the stairs to my bedroom to change into something a bit dressier.

My whole body was tingling. If I had been a dog, my ears would be pricked up, waiting for the sound of the doorbell that would mean Nick was there to walk me over to his apartment.

Who was I kidding? It totally felt like a date.

CHAPTER 2

I probably should have given it a second before opening the door when Nick rang the bell. Taken a breath first or something. It didn't help that a sudden gust of wind ripped the door from my hands so that it hit the foyer wall with a bang.

"Well," Nick said. As startled as he was, he was still a Minnesotan.

"You look..." I hadn't meant to start that thought out loud. But the cold wind had brought a flush to his cheeks that somehow made his eyes seem brighter than usual. Now my stomach was doing something besides growling. I focused on some other way to end that sentence and noticed the orange hunting cap, flaps pulled down low over his ears. "Warm," I said.

"It's freezing out here," he said. "We should shut that door." He started to step in, but I thrust the covered plate of pumpkin pie cupcakes into his hands.

"I'm all ready to go," I said, pulling the door shut behind me. Ready to go, and eager to get out of there before Sophie could possibly be drawn by the noise.

Did I think she would embarrass me? No.

But I wasn't willing to bet on that.

My new wool coat was pleasantly warm, and the lined leather

gloves were like a dream. I was used to hand-knit mittens and not having the use of my fingers outdoors for three months of the year. But with the gloves, I had no problem catching the end of my soft scarf and drawing it up over my head to keep my ears out of the wind.

"You look fancy," Nick said. Then his cheeks flushed a deeper shade of red. He must be picking up old-fashioned words living with his grandfather.

"I do," I said merrily. "Apparently, our inheritance of the school includes a monthly allowance, and when we got it, Sophie insisted I spend mine on a whole new wardrobe."

"That must have been fun," he said. There was just a hint of a question mark on the end of that sentence.

"I'm not really a shopping girl," I said, confirming his suspicion, I was sure. "I like nice things; I just don't like the process of finding them. And Sophie took me to the Mall of America. Have you ever been there?"

"Once or twice," Nick said.

"It's really big and really full of people," I said. "It's kind of stressful."

"But the mission was a success?" he said.

"Actually, it was," I said. "I think it's part of Sophie's magic, finding the perfect thing among racks and racks of the wrong things. That, and the thing where she can make her hair look perfect just by running her fingers through it."

Nick cleared his throat awkwardly. I'm guessing it was the word "magic." I had explained to him that we were witches, but only the barest of details. He reacted badly to me trying to tell him more than he was ready to hear. Apparently, even the stray mention was almost painful for him.

"Here we are," he said, rushing up the steps of the condo building to hold the door open for me. I stepped past him, unwinding the scarf from around my head.

The lobby had the feeling of a place designed for a use it never saw. The benches against the far wall didn't look like they'd ever been sat on. But someone spent time here. The elaborate brass art thing on the wall, some radiating wires with knobbier bits that spanned more than four feet, was completely free of dust.

"We're upstairs," Nick said, moving the plate of cupcakes from hand to hand as he pulled off his gloves with his teeth.

"How many units are there?" I asked as I followed him down a long hallway lit by bright lights that hung down from the ceiling like globes from metallic stems.

"Eight," he said. "Four up and four down. The two at the back upstairs have a partial river view, but grandfather and I are in the unit at the front."

The hallway ended in a glass-walled stairwell. The steps were wide but shallow, and so thickly carpeted our feet made no sound. Nick smiled back at me from the landing before continuing up the second flight of steps to the second floor.

"I should warn you about the food," Nick was saying. "My grandfather has been a widower since he was forty. He loves to cook, but I'm not sure everyone would call what he does cooking. It's basically opening a lot of cans and adding a top layer of potato chips before throwing it in the oven."

"Comfort food," I said with a smile. "I'm sure it will be just fine."

"I should have asked if you were a vegetarian or anything," he said.

"Total omnivore," I said. I was going to say something more, but out of nowhere I had a sudden, vicious pain in my head. More than a headache; it was as if my head were being cleaved in two by an axe.

The world went black around me, and the ringing in my ears drowned out Nick's voice to nothing more than a concerned-sounding murmur in a cacophony of bells. I felt something hit my knees and was vaguely aware that I had fallen forward.

I put both my hands to my head, trying to somehow hold it all together. It wanted to fall apart, to fall open and expose my brain. The open air on my brain, that was going to be intolerable. Like when you get an injection with a needle and somehow taste steel on your tongue. Too, too much sensation.

Then, as promptly as it started, it was gone.

"Amanda?"

"I'm okay," I said, but I was still clutching my head. I forced my hands to unclench from my hair. The hair I had been so careful not to muss by forgoing a hat and being gentle with the scarf. It would be a chaotic mess now.

"Are you sure?" Nick asked. He had dropped to one knee beside me. I wasn't sure he was even aware that he was still holding a plate of cupcakes.

"Yes," I said, taking a shaky breath, then another, steadier one. "Yes, it's passed."

"What was it?"

"I don't know," I said. "I've never felt anything like that before."

"Is it a side effect from what happened to you before? The poisoning?" he asked.

"After all this time? I don't think so," I said. "I could use a drink of water, though."

"Of course," he said, getting to his feet, then extending his free hand to help me back to mine. I smoothed the end of my tunic sweater back down over my leggings and summoned a reassuring smile. "I'm fine."

"Tell me if that changes," he said earnestly.

"I will," I promised. But I doubted I would get a warning the second time when I hadn't had one the first time.

A wink of light caught my eye, the brass numbers on the door of the condo on my right. The one with a river view.

I had a sudden urge to throw open that door, to enter the apartment beyond and face whatever had just triggered what I had gone through. But that made no sense. There was no sound from the other side of the door, and no light coming from under the door itself.

"Who lives here?" I asked. Nick looked up at the number as he held out his arm for me to take. An old-fashioned gesture, but not one I was prepared to refuse.

"There? I've never seen anyone go in or out of there," he admitted. "There aren't any vacancies in the building. I guess it must be snowbirds."

Nick guided me down the hall to the last door on the right. He knocked lightly before opening the door. He immediately stuck out one knee, a gesture that struck me as rather strange until his grandfather's Irish setter Finnegan charged into it.

"Hey, buddy," Nick said, handing me the plate of cupcakes so he could scratch Finnegan's ears then catch hold of his collar to direct him out of the doorway.

"Nick?" a voice called from further in the apartment.

"Hey, granddad," Nick called back. "We're here."

I stepped into the apartment. My first impression was all gleaming white and darkest black in boxy, mostly horizontal arrangements. The building had a modernist design to it, and Nick's granddad followed that up with a few modernist pieces of furniture but a mostly minimalist feel. No art on the bright white walls, no visible hardware on the dark black wood of the cabinet doors that matched the hardwood floor.

Nick's grandfather was emerging from the kitchen that was set off from the living room by a bar of the same dark wood. He was wiping his hands on a kitchen towel.

"Hello, Mr. Larson," I said, putting out my hand to shake. "I'm Amanda Clarke."

"So good to meet you," he said. He gave my hand a quick shake, then raised it to his lips to brush the back of it with a dry kiss. "Nick has told me quite a bit about you."

"Likewise," I said, then held out the plate. "I brought dessert. Pumpkin pie cupcakes. I know Thanksgiving is almost here, but I just can't wait for pumpkin pie."

"I'm quite the fan of it myself," he said with a wink. He took the plate with him back to the kitchen.

Dinner was all Nick had told me it would be: tuna casserole topped with what I was sure were Old Dutch potato chips, and even the peas had come from a can.

I loved it. It was a far cry from Mr. Trevor's carefully executed recipes, but it tasted like stick-to-your-ribs food. Food to eat with a family.

Nick's granddad talked through the entire meal, anecdotes of

Nick's childhood that seemed designed to bring that blush back to Nick's cheeks. I laughed and prompted him to tell me more in all the appropriate places, but in truth, I was having a hard time concentrating.

It was like that apartment next door was looming over me. Casting a shadow on my mind. I didn't sense a consciousness, or I didn't think I did. I was still new to this whole magic thing.

But something was demanding my attention. What could it be?

"We should have some coffee with these cupcakes," Nick's granddad said.

"You sit. I'll get it," Nick said, putting a hand on his granddad's shoulder as if he might have to use force to keep him in place.

"He's a good boy," he said when Nick was occupied with the coffeemaker.

"He is," I agreed.

"He's seen things he can't unsee. He doesn't talk about it, but I can tell. I saw some things myself, back when I was in Vietnam," he said. He stopped talking with something like a lurch, like he hadn't meant to open this line of dialogue at all but couldn't find a way out of it now.

"Do you know who lives next door to you?" I asked, tipping my head towards the apartment in question.

The apartment glowered back at me. I ignored it.

"Next door?" he repeated. He took a minute to reorient himself after my drastic change of topic, then sat back in his chair and folded his arms over his chest. "I can't recall their name, actually. They bought their unit when the building was still under construction, but by the time I moved in, they were no longer using it. I reckon they still own it, but they're never here. One of those ridiculously wealthy families that just collect property all over the world, I suppose."

"So, the apartment itself is empty?" I asked. "No one is subletting it or anything?"

"No, no subletting in this building," he said with a frown. "I haven't the foggiest idea what it looks like in there. Sad, really. It has one of the nicer views, or so the building manager tells me."

Nick rejoined us with the coffee and cupcakes on a tray, and the conversation turned to me and my back story.

Once you take the magic out, my back story is really very sparse. It didn't even last so long as the coffee.

"I should get going," I said.

"So soon?" Nick's grandfather said sadly.

"Please excuse me, I'm really not feeling myself tonight," I said. "I had the strangest of headaches before. It's gone now, but I feel a bit out of sorts."

"You'll have to come back on another night when you're feeling more up to it," he said, as if this were a statement of fact and not an invitation. "It's generally just Nick and me with old Finnegan here. Your company brings a light to this gloomy place."

He was being kind. Distracted as I was, I doubted I had contributed anything much to the little party. But I smiled and thanked him.

"Let me grab my coat, and I'll walk you back," Nick said.

"Oh no," I said, far too quickly. He looked struck, then confused.

Wait, had he thought this was a date as well? Did he think walking me back to the house was part of the night?

Oh, how I wanted him to walk me back. To linger on the porch. No, scratch that, to linger in the foyer. The wind outside was really too much.

But I wanted something even more than that, sadly. I wanted to snoop around that apartment. And I couldn't do that with Nick with me. He really didn't like it when I bent or broke the law.

"No, it's all right," I said. "It's my head. I think I need a bit of a walk to clear it. A walk alone. I'm sorry."

"Don't be," Nick said. We stopped at the apartment door, and he looked at me, hand on the doorknob without opening it. "You're sure you're okay?"

"I'll feel better after a walk and a good night's sleep," I said.

"Okay," he said with palpable reluctance. "Text me when you get home. And text me in the morning to let me know how you're feeling."

"I will," I promised.

It took him a moment, but eventually, he stopped looking at me and opened the door.

"Good night," I said.

"Good night, Amanda," he said.

I was afraid he was going to watch me walk all the way down the hall, and I would have to wait for the door to close before sneaking back. Then I was afraid he was watching me, not out of politeness but to be sure that I didn't do exactly what I was about to do. Did he know me so well?

Whether he did or didn't, in the end, Finnegan finally saw the door standing open and made another dash for it. Nick caught him just in time, the door swinging shut as he cajoled the dog.

I waited a moment to be sure he wasn't going to open the door again, but nothing disturbed the heavy silence of the hallway. Nothing but the wind gusting against the glass around the stairwell.

I turned my attention to the door of the empty apartment. What clue could I possibly hope to find?

But any clue at all was better than no clue.

CHAPTER 3

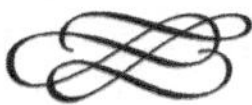

I stood in front of the heavy fireproof door, looking up at the brass numbers and the tiny dot that was the peephole. It seemed to be towering over me, like the massive gates into the forbidden castle in a fantasy story.

It was just a door and a door of ordinary dimensions at that. But with no way for me to get past it, I guess it was for all intents and purposes an impregnable gate.

I did entertain the notion of breaking in. Only I had no idea how to do that. Lock-picking wasn't an elective when I was in high school. Brianna might know a spell to make locks open, but I didn't.

But there was one thing I could do.

I reached out my hands to press my palms to the door, hesitating just before they made contact. What if I had that sudden rush of head pain again? What if it was worse this time?

I bit down on my lip and pushed that thought aside. If it came back, I'd deal with it. That was all.

I pressed my hands to the door. The steel was numbingly cold under my hands, but I didn't draw back. Instead, I leaned forward until my forehead, too, was pressed to the cold metal.

Then I closed my eyes and forced my breathing into a slow, even rhythm.

The only times I had shifted my perception into the world of interconnecting energy had been under great duress, and I had done it largely instinctually. Now, while I stood in more or less complete safety, I wasn't sure how to move myself over.

But I remember how it had felt, and how it had looked. I concentrated on that while maintaining my breathing.

It took a long time, but finally I felt a little different, a little removed from my body. I opened my eyes and saw the webs of energy all around me.

I had done it! I was getting better at this magic thing after all!

I forced myself to stay on task and focused again on the door I was touching. I examined every energy thread, every node that made up the door. But I could see nothing unusual. There was no sign of anything out of the ordinary about the door or up or down the hallway.

I shifted my perception, passing my awareness through the door into the apartment beyond. Still, all the threads looked perfectly ordinary. I didn't have more than a vague sense of what I was looking at, how it correlated to the real world, but I decided that all I was seeing was the patterns created by bare walls and empty floors. No living things here.

Not only was the apartment unoccupied, it was completely empty.

Wait, not completely. I sensed something a little deeper in, an object that was as tall as I was but rectangular in shape.

This wasn't exactly ordinary. The threads shone differently. Brighter.

I examined it thread by thread. It didn't seem to be aware of my presence, and it didn't radiate menace as the crystal ball had the last time I was in the web world.

So, not evil, but definitely not ordinary. Did that make it a magical object or not? I supposed there might be ways to be out of the ordinary without being magical. But I didn't know how specifically, or what it might mean. I just didn't have enough experience in correlating the web world to the real world.

I fell back into my body with a rush, staggering back from the door. My ears were throbbing, and my chest had a tingling feeling to it, and I was sucking in deep lungfuls of air as if I had gone without for far too long.

As the lightheadedness passed, I realized that was probably exactly what had happened. I hadn't been aware enough of my own body to keep it breathing, or to sense that it wasn't while I was poking around the webs inside the apartment.

Would I have been forced back into my body when I fainted from lack of oxygen?

Or what if I didn't? What if I died while my consciousness was exploring the world of webs? Would I become a ghost, doomed to haunt the other world forever?

Or would I just wink out of existence?

I pulled myself together, wrapping my scarf around my head as I headed down the stairs and out the door.

In the future, it would be a good idea to have a spotter while I tried such things. At least until I understood it all better.

It felt like a lifetime had passed since I had left the house, but it was still early evening yet when I blew in with the wind and wrestled that heavy door shut. I threw aside my coat and scarf and went straight up to the library to find Brianna.

She was, as always, at the table that was the very heart of the library amid a towering sprawl of books and countless abandoned cups of tea. It looked like I had caught her at the perfect moment, as she was not currently engrossed in either reading from one of the massive tomes or writing away inside her own journal. She was on her feet, moving around the periphery of the table, looking at each of the books as if hunting for something.

"Can I help?" I asked.

"No, I've got it. "She didn't look up at me, just continued her search. She dug one book out from the middle of a stack and paged through it excitedly. Then her face fell, and she set it back down and resumed her search.

"Well, if you have a moment, I could use some help," I said.

"Really don't," she said.

"It's just, something weird just happened. I think I had some kind of episode? I don't know what it was," I said.

Brianna made a little murmuring sound that could mean anything or nothing at all. She pulled out another book and examined the cover closely, running her fingers over the embossed type.

"I don't know what just happened to me," I went on. "I thought maybe something was attacking me, but I don't sense any danger."

"Yeah," Brianna said absently, either to me or to the book.

"I tried looking in the web world. I couldn't find anything odd. Although apparently, I have to learn how to keep myself breathing while I'm in the web world. I didn't expect that to be a thing."

Brianna looked up at me sharply. "You astrally projected?"

"Did I?" I had no idea what exactly that meant.

"You astrally projected without protecting your physical form first?"

"I guess maybe?" I said.

"Either you did, or you didn't," Brianna said.

"How can I tell?" I asked.

"Ugh, Amanda!" Brianna said, circling the table to drop the book she was holding next to her journal. "I pulled every conceivable book I could find in this library about anything related to the sort of magic you said you could do. Didn't you read any of them?"

"I tried," I said, not meeting her eyes. "They were big books. Most of it didn't sound like what I did, so..."

"So you gave up," Brianna said with a sigh. "After what, four books? Five?"

I said nothing.

The correct answer was two.

"I even flagged the ones I thought you should start with, the more generalized ones. I know the very top book covered the dangers of astral projection. You did read it, didn't you?"

"I tried," I said lamely.

"Amanda, honestly!" Brianna said, throwing up her hands. She looked so frustrated, as if she were about to start crying. The atmosphere in the library was suddenly getting very uncomfortable. "I try to help you out as much as I can, but it just never feels like you're doing your part."

"I'm way behind you and Sophie in learning this stuff," I said. "It's only been a couple of months."

"But you don't seem to be trying," Brianna said. "I have so much to go through here. It's completely overwhelming, and then you are constantly wanting me to help you. And it's not just pointing you in the right direction. You want me to hold your hand every step of the way. To stand behind you while you read and explain every single thing."

"I'm not that bad," I said.

"Amanda, I'm not going to be able to master your power for you. I don't know a thing about it. It's a very rare sort of magic. And I can't really know what's useful to you because I don't have your perspective of actually having the power and seeing the world your way. I can't master a power I don't even possess and then teach it to you. I just can't. I can't do it."

"Okay, okay," I said, holding up my hands as if I could stave off Brianna's impending emotional collapse.

"I have so much work to do!" she all but wailed, gesturing vaguely at the mountain of books on the table.

"I'm sorry," I said. "It's okay. I'll figure it out. Somehow."

She was still talking, rambling on and on, but this time just to herself. Somehow that involved more facial expressions and gestures than she used when talking to others. It was kind of scary to watch, like she was going to have a complete mental break at any moment.

But there was nothing I could do but make things worse, so I quietly retreated from the library. I thought about making her more tea and bringing it up as a peace offering, but then her monologue kicked up to a hysterical level, and I thought it best to just leave her be.

I could sneak in through the other door and get to the little table in the back that was my workstation, where all the books Brianna had found for me were arrayed in neat stacks, largely undisturbed since she had put them there.

But I doubted I would find them any more enlightening than I had before. It was a shame no one had done any YouTube channels on channeling one's rare time magic or understanding the world when you perceived it as a web of energy and threads that joined to tell stories. That might be really helpful.

But alas, I was stuck with musty all books written in antiquated English with far too many asides in French, Latin, and Greek.

Emotional outbursts aside, I knew Brianna's frustration wasn't so much that I was interrupting her as that she really wasn't able to help me. She really couldn't understand my magic, and I couldn't explain it well enough for her to grasp it. She really, truly wanted to help me. She just couldn't.

I don't think it was a feeling she was used to. She clearly didn't like it. I felt bad for her.

Which I guess is a little weird. I was the one who needed help, and yet I felt sympathy for her because she couldn't help me.

But then, I had other avenues to getting help. I wasn't having a book problem, after all. I was having a problem understanding what I was feeling and perceiving. And that was really more Sophie's domain, anyway.

Surely Sophie wouldn't mind having her evening interrupted.

CHAPTER 4

After searching the rest of the house and even going back out into the wind to look in the cellar, I finally found Sophie in the attic.

Just where I had left her. I probably should have started there, logically. I guess my encounter with Brianna had left me more rattled than I had thought.

I had put on a hoodie before going out into the backyard to check the cellar, and I was still wearing it as I climbed the steps to the attic. Good thing, too. Even though Sophie was still in that space, she was no longer warming it with scent-laden New Orleans breezes. It was, in fact, quite cold.

But apparently, that was deliberate, for whatever reason. Sophie was wearing a warmup jacket over her normal clothes. Although it had no team name on the back, it reminded me of what the dancers in my high school had worn from time to time. She even had old school leg warmers pulled up over the calves of her skinny jeans, slouching low over her canvas shoes. A fuzzy headband sat low on her head to cover her ears.

If I tried to wear a band like that, it would make my hair jut up like the bride of Frankenstein. But not Sophie. Her bangs were pushed back from her forehead but in a perfect pompadour wave.

Honestly, I don't know how she ever got through life without everyone knowing she was a witch. Her hair game just wasn't natural.

She was turned mostly away from me as I approached the doorway and I stopped just short of going into the room. I admit I was a little gun-shy about interrupting and breaking her focus. Clearly, I had been wrong about how engrossed in her task Brianna had been. I kept still so I wouldn't distract Sophie out of the corner of her eye.

She had her own eyes closed, though, and looked like she was murmuring something to herself. Then she straightened her back and raised her wand. She moved it slowly through the air in a long loop, creating another ribbon, this one of a lovely dusky rose color. It seemed to be having trouble streaming out of the end of the wand, however. It bunched and knotted, and Sophie's little shaking gestures with her wand weren't helping it get loose.

Then she made a sweeping gesture with her other hand, a long motion that started under the elbow of her wand hand, then extended out and up, ending in a delicate pose with her elbow up but her hand behind her head.

The ribbon ruffled out of the wand tip and spread out full-length parallel to the floor. It rippled as if in a breeze, and for just a second, I once more smelled jasmine with hints of coffee and pastries.

Then Sophie gave a loud groan of frustration and even stamped a foot. She brought both of her arms down with a cutting gesture, and the ribbon didn't crumble to pretty bits like before.

It caught fire and exploded.

Which I thought was really impressive, but Sophie was stomping around, perhaps partly to warm her feet but clearly mainly in anger about something.

She took a deep breath and went back to the center of the room, closing her eyes to try again. Again the ribbon started to form but then just hung wrapped around the tip, unable to pull free. This time she raised both of her arms at once, and when she followed through on that motion by rising up on her toes ribbon after ribbon started flying out of the end of her wand, all dancing around the attic like a family of long-tailed birds.

But Sophie's frustration this time wasn't so much a groan as a scream, and she flung both of her arms wide, blasting the entire room with a hot wind that dripped with humidity and reeked of urine and vomit.

I was caught off guard and took too deep of a breath of that noxious mix and found myself coughing. Sophie spun to face me, her face flushing darkly.

Ooh, she was angry. I suddenly knew how those ribbons felt. If I could set myself on fire and explode just to make her shift her gaze away from me, I would.

"Sorry, sorry," I said, still coughing at the thick reek of the air. "I didn't mean to interrupt. You looked like you were doing well a second ago."

"I was not," Sophie said. As usual, when her emotions were high, her Creole accent was thicker. "I was cheating."

"Cheating? How can you cheat with magic?" I asked.

"I'm meant to be using the wand as a focus," Sophie said, glaring at the wand in her hand. "But instead I keep shifting back to dance magic. What I already know. I'll never get stronger if I don't stop doing the easy thing."

"You might be being a little hard on yourself," I said, then almost flinched as that gaze swept back up on me.

"Why are you here?" Sophie asked.

"I wanted…" I stammered, then fell silent. Nothing on earth was going to make me say the word 'help' now. I started again. "I wanted to consult with you on a matter."

"Consult," Sophie repeated. She was getting calmer. She never did stay angry for long, but I was still nervous.

"I felt something weird when I was in the building next door," I said. "I tried some of the meditation techniques you taught me, and I managed to get into the altered state where I can perceive the web world without being forced into it by nearly dying."

I paused, a part of me hoping she would be impressed. But she just looked at me, waiting for me to continue.

"The problem was I stayed in that state too long, and I wasn't paying enough attention to my body," I said. "Brianna called it astral projection? Do you know what that is?"

"Roughly," Sophie said with a shrug.

"Ah," I said. "Have you ever done it?"

"No," Sophie said. For some reason, that seemed to make her frustrated again, like I was pointing out another limitation to her magic. Which I absolutely wasn't doing, but there didn't seem to be any way to say that without, in fact, pointing in that direction.

So I pressed on. "I'm hoping we can work on some techniques together."

Sophie sighed and pressed a hand to her forehead, knocking the headband askew.

"When you have time," I rushed to add. "I just need someone to watch my body while I try moving over to that other place. The web world. To be sure I'm safe."

"What good would that do?" Sophie asked.

I suspected a trap. There was an edge to her voice that said any answer I gave to that was going to be a wrong one. But I gave it a shot. "Once I work out the basics with your..."—not help—"assistance, I should be able to take it from there."

"Will you?" Sophie said.

"Yes," I said.

"Will you really? You're going to practice? Really practice?"

"Yes," I said again.

"Well, that would be lovely to see," Sophie said.

"I practice," I said. Even to my own ears, I sounded sullen.

"When one of us stands over you, yes, I guess you practice," Sophie said.

"I practice on my own too," I said. Now I was starting to get annoyed.

"Not much," Sophie shot back.

"I do too," I said. "How would you know if you're not there?"

"Because when someone practices, they get better at things. And not just the easy things. They get better at the hard things," she said.

"I'm at a disadvantage," I said. "I started years behind you and Brianna."

"So we're all very aware," Sophie said.

"Maybe we should talk about this some other time," I said, taking half a step back.

"Yes, run along. Catch me or Brianna when we're in a better mood and coax us into doing all the heavy lifting for you again."

I literally bit my tongue. I didn't want to get into a fight. But it really felt like Sophie was attacking me out of nowhere. She and Brianna had always been so supportive of the fact that, unlike them, I hadn't grown up knowing about the existence of magic. I didn't have the background to easily pick these things up now. But I was trying. I was struggling, but I was always trying.

"Is this some weird spell?" I murmured to myself. "You're both acting so strangely."

"We're both past the point of carrying your weight, and you find that strange?" Sophie asked.

"No, not that," I said, scrambling to regain control of the conversation. "I just felt something strange when I was at Nick's place, a sudden pain in my head out of nowhere. It went away just as suddenly as it came, but it was so intense when it happened it really felt like an attack."

"If someone were attacking you, why would they just stop?" Sophie asked. Her anger was shifting back down to annoyance and frustration, but I could deal with those.

"I don't know what it was. That's what I'm trying to figure out, what it was. I went into the web world to see if anything looked magical or malignant or whatever. But I don't really know enough about how that world works in relation to this one to be sure of anything. I mean, I saw something there, but I don't know what it was."

"And this was next door?" Sophie asked.

"In the building next door, on the second floor in the back," I said.

Sophie half-closed her eyes for a moment, and I imagined she was reaching out with her senses. Maybe she would feel it too, what I had felt when I had peaked inside the empty apartment.

But Sophie just opened her eyes again and looked straight at me as she tucked her wand away behind her.

"It's nothing," she said.

"Nothing?"

"Nothing to do with us," she clarified. "The time bridge is exactly as it should be. Nothing is moving through it; nothing is being affected by it."

"But I didn't think this was related to the time bridge," I said.

"Then we *really* don't need to worry about it," Sophie said.

"But it still might be magic," I insisted.

"We have a calling," Sophie said, leaving the attic to stand toe to toe with me at the top of the stairs. "We have a mission. One only we can do. That calling is not to control all magic in the known world. It's to maintain that passage through time, to stand as gatekeepers between 1927 and today. Maybe what you perceived was a magic thing. The world is full of magic things. The vast, vast majority of them are no business of ours."

Sophie brushed past me to head down the stairs, but I just couldn't let it go.

"What if something really was attacking me?" I asked.

She paused at the landing but didn't look back up at me. "If you think you're in danger going to Nick's place, the answer is very simple. Don't go to Nick's."

Then she went down the rest of the stairs and disappeared on the third floor.

I had the urge to just sit down where I was, to slump into a fugue state there at the top of the steps and just never come out of it.

But it was far too cold for that. I huddled down deeper inside my hoodie and headed down the stairs myself.

CHAPTER 5

I went into my bedroom and shut the door, still half entertaining the notion of settling into a fugue state either in the chair by the fireplace or maybe just in the bed—in which case we could just call it sleep—when I gave a strangled gasp and fell to my knees.

It wasn't my head this time. No sensation of having to hold my skull together. No, this time it was like a line of fire stretched across my throat, burning deeper into my neck even as my hands reached up to close around it. To hold something in.

Blood, I suppose. My hands felt wet and sticky, as if coated by a hot spray.

I didn't want to look.

But I couldn't keep my eyes closed tight forever. Not that having them open was going to show me any way to help my situation. I was rapidly running out of breath, my throat unable to pass any air through to my lungs.

It felt a bit like drowning and a bit like being strangled both at once.

The floor slammed into me, and I realized I had fallen to my side.

Then I did open my eyes and found myself back in the world of webs. I couldn't draw a breath, but in this place, I didn't need to.

I turned to look down at my own body, but the threads that ran through it were all entirely normal. As far as I could tell, there was nothing wrong with me. No injury, no spell. And yet, clearly, something was happening.

I looked around, but the house around me was almost blinding in its dense network of connections. It was filled with magic, yes, but it was more than that. It was as if the house existed in every time at once, and I saw them all overlapping each other, adding their brightness to each other.

It was too much. I turned my attention back to my body and was about to attempt to settle back into it when something else commanded my attention.

I looked towards the building next door, thinking it was the object in the empty apartment that was calling me, but that wasn't it. It was something closer, inside the house. Not in my room or on my floor, but close.

Then my eyes were opening, my real eyes, and I pushed myself up off of the hardwood floor.

I was going to have a bruise, I was sure. My shoulder and ribs were protesting that fall.

I sat up straighter, listening for the sound of running footsteps. I thought I had cried out when the pain struck me. I knew there would have been a thump when I fell. But no one was coming to investigate.

Well, whatever.

I got back to my feet, then headed back down the hallway, moving slowly as my sore body protested, but the aches were already fading. Just another illusion.

Now, where had that thing been that had called out to me? Below me, but just a bit. Inside the house. I went to the stairs and slipped down to the second floor, careful not to make any sound as I crept past the open doors to the library.

Another door was also open: the door to Miss Zenobia's office. I didn't know if Mr. Trevor kept it locked or not. I had assumed locked, but then I had never tried to go in there. I hadn't had any reason to. I had certainly never seen that door just standing open.

But it was as if it were inviting me in.

I paused in the doorway and fumbled for the light switch. Everything was just as it had been the last time I had been in this office. When the ghost of Miss Zenobia Weekes had spoken to the three of us. When I had learned that I was a witch.

Wait, I had been in here once since then. The day Brianna and Sophie had tried to trigger my magic by attacking me.

Well, in that case, someone had done an epic level of cleaning up. But then, with how Mr. Trevor revered Miss Zenobia's memory, that was perhaps to be expected. Still, we had done some heavy damage. Some things were missing, but most were back as they had been. I was impressed.

I walked around the room, hands clasped behind my back. Something had called me here, but I also remembered Mr. Trevor's warning about not touching things. And I had seen what chaos some of these objects could unleash just by brushing up against one or lifting the lid of another. Better safe than sorry.

I found myself sitting down in Miss Zenobia's velvet-cushioned chair, running my hands over the lovingly maintained surface of the ancient desk. For a moment I could almost sense her there, the smell of her like lavender. The gruffness of her voice.

Then I opened the pencil drawer over my knees and saw that it contained a single key that glowed golden in the light. It was a modern-looking key, but featureless. Like the blanks they have in hardware stores that you can use to make copies of your own keys.

I had never seen a skeleton key before. I didn't know if this was that or not. But I picked it up, stuck it in my pocket, and went back downstairs to get my coat.

I didn't want to think too much about what might be guiding me. I rather wished it was part of my own power, like the feelings I sometimes got that meant I just had to do something or not do something else.

But this didn't feel quite like that, and I was a little afraid that somehow Juno might be involved. Manipulating me. But it didn't feel like her either.

There was still so much about magic that I didn't yet understand.

The key got me into the lobby of the building. Then it got me past that cold metal door into the empty apartment.

The design was similar to Nick's grandfather's apartment, with white walls and dark wood floors and trim, but the overhead light wouldn't come on when I flipped the switch. The only illumination was from the light outside set over the condo's parking lot, and that mostly lit up the ceiling. I could see dust everywhere, cobwebs so long and dust-coated they looked fake.

I walked past the kitchen area, down the hallway, past the main bathroom and two small bedrooms. Everything was empty.

Then I got to the end of the hallway, to the master bedroom. The far wall was one long, narrow window. It looked like it was designed to frame the panorama of its river view and eliminate everything above and below that. It seemed a bit restrictive to me, and it wasn't allowing in much light.

But the room was lit well enough for me to see that it wasn't quite empty. Against the wall to my right was a very distinctly unmodern wardrobe. It was hard to tell when everything was covered in a blanket of dust, but I got the sense that it might be a genuine antique. It looked like the sort of thing they would've had in Versailles back in the day.

I walked over to it, clutching the key tightly in my hand as if it were some sort of talisman and could keep me safe.

I reached out a hand slowly, muscles tensed in case I needed to pull it away in a hurry, like someone trying to see if an iron was on and ready by risking a touch to its surface.

I brushed a fingertip over the door's knob. Nothing happened. I used two fingers to gently tug it open, then stepped back as the door swung wide.

I had a brief glimpse of a perfectly ordinary, perfectly empty wardrobe.

Then I was on my knees again. Something hit my chest that felt like being kicked by a cow, and there was a burning sensation spreading through my chest.

Then I was hit again and again. I fell to the floor, trying to wrap myself up into a tight ball, but all that did was change the point of impact from my chest to the area over my kidneys.

Then, just like that, it was over. The pain was gone.

Well, the stabbing pain was gone. I was gathering quite the collection of aches from all the falling to the floor I was doing this evening.

I pushed myself up to a sitting position and brushed the hair back out of my eyes.

And saw the body in the wardrobe.

It definitely hadn't been there a moment before. I was sure of that. I had seen the empty wardrobe. I had seen every pattern to the wood that was its bottom. There hadn't been anything in it.

But now there was a man curled up in there, knees drawn up tight as if he too had been fending off blows to his chest.

And he was bleeding. Even in the dim light, I could see the dark patches all over his clothes, across his chest, and on his back over his kidneys. As I watched, it formed an ever-expanding pool on the bottom of the wardrobe, then started dripping down to the floor itself.

I reached in to touch him. If he was still bleeding, he might be still breathing.

But he was not. Glassy eyes gazed up at me, and I felt no pulse, no heartbeat.

But he was still warm.

I hadn't moved him much—he was a big man and rather heavy—but I had jostled him enough to dislodge his hat. It fell out of the wardrobe and rolled across the floor. I bent to pick it up, then held it up in the brightest bit of light from the window.

I had seen hats like this before. Lots of them.

In 1927.

It could be a coincidence. The man in the wardrobe could be a hipster, or just like old hats.

But the more I looked at him, even in the scant light that penetrated the wardrobe, I saw that all his clothes were old-fashioned.

I might have still been able to tell myself it was all a coincidence. Sophie had said the time bridge was undisturbed; it had to be a coincidence.

Except I knew for a fact that before I had felt myself stabbed, that wardrobe had been empty.

I set the hat back on his head, then stepped back from the wardrobe. What was I going to do now?

"Hello?" a voice called from the door of the apartment.

The door I had left standing open.

I looked around and briefly considered hiding in the walk-in closet. But I knew it wouldn't do any good.

Because that voice was Nick's. He was going to investigate. He was going to find me. And he was going to be mad.

But maybe, just maybe, he would be ever so slightly less mad if I didn't look like I was guiltily hiding myself.

Maybe.

CHAPTER 6

Unlike me, Nick had planned ahead. Nick had a flashlight.
I resisted the urge to put my hands up when he shone it on me.

"Amanda? Was that you I heard a minute ago?"

Oh, so I was yelling out loud when I was in pain. Good to know.

"I think so," I said.

"What are you doing in here anyway?" he asked.

"I went home, but I felt another sudden attack of pain, like I had in the hallway just outside this door. I thought they might be connected. I came over to be sure," I said.

"This is a magic thing?" he asked. Or whispered, really.

"It's definitely a magic thing," I said.

Then he finally saw the body in the wardrobe.

"Amanda!" he cried, looking from the body to me with eyes wide.

"He was dead before... I saw him," I finished lamely. I could scarcely claim he was dead before I opened the wardrobe. I was pretty sure that wasn't true.

"Who is he?" Nick asked, shining his light on the man's face.

"I'm not sure," I said. "I don't really know what's going on here. Not yet, anyway."

"Not yet? What are you planning to do here?" he demanded.

"Nothing!" I insisted. "I didn't know there was a dead man in here when I came inside the apartment. I just knew there was a thing which turned out to be this wardrobe."

"A magic thing?"

"I guess. I don't know. I'm still working on it," I said.

"You can't be in here," Nick said, catching hold of my arm and steering me back towards the apartment door. "It's a crime scene."

"It's not a crime the police are going to solve," I said.

"Not another one!" he said.

"I'm not making it happen," I said.

"Aren't you?" he asked. "I mean, I know not deliberately. But you sure seem to attract trouble. And dead bodies."

"Only since I moved here," I said.

"If you didn't know there was a dead body in here, why did you break in?" Nick asked.

"I wanted to take a look at the wardrobe," I said.

"So you knew about the wardrobe?"

"I knew there was something that turned out to be a wardrobe, yes," I said. I tried to summon a grin, but he wasn't having it.

"We've talked about this before. Probable cause. You didn't have it. You just committed a crime. Maybe not murder, but breaking and entering."

"Maybe not murder?" I repeated incredulously.

"You know what I mean!" he snapped, then took a calming breath. "Look, you can't keep turning up at crime scenes."

"I'm not trying to," I said.

"How did you even get in here?" he asked.

I opened my hand and showed him the golden key resting on my palm.

"A skeleton key wouldn't work on this kind of lock," he said dully.

"No, I suppose not," I said and put the key into my pocket.

"Rules just don't apply to you, do they?" he sighed.

"I obey the rules, most of the time," I said. "Look, three times I felt like someone was attacking me. Cracking my skull, slitting my throat, stabbing me all over my body. If you felt something like that, you'd want to get to the bottom of it too."

"That man was stabbed, but his head and his throat are fine. What does that mean?" he asked.

"I don't know," I said. "I really don't. I'm still investigating."

"Snooping," he said. "You really can't be here."

"That man's body doesn't belong here," I told him.

"In this apartment?"

"In 2018," I said.

He actually flinched.

"If you look at his clothes..."

"Stop," he said, his tone very carefully controlled. "Just stop."

"The police are not going to know what to do with this," I said.

"And yet that's their job," he said. "And I'm going to have to call them. Again. I certainly hope no one is tracking all the open cases with my name attached. I'll graduate from police academy with too much suspicious stuff in my background to be hireable."

"You don't have to call them," I said. "I can do it. I'll take the heat."

"Forget it," he said. "It's right next door to me. There's no way I'm not getting swept up in this."

"I can point them another way..."

"Just forget it," he said, more firmly. "I've got this. Just take that key, whatever it is, and get out of here. I guess I'll say I heard someone cry out in pain and came over to investigate. That much of it has the advantage of actually being true."

"Nick," I said.

But he just turned away from me, already pulling out his cell phone.

"I'm sorry," I whispered. I don't know if he heard me. He immediately started talking to the dispatcher.

I slipped out of the apartment, back into the darkness and the wind.

When I came in the front door of Miss Zenobia's house, I saw the light was on in the kitchen. I wasn't remotely hungry—that tuna casserole was sticking with me—but I rather hoped I'd run into Mr.

Trevor tottering about back there. I could really use a friendly face, someone that was happy to see me.

But it was Sophie and Brianna, both eating a late supper. Brianna had a plate piled with buttered toast and Sophie was eating some left-over chicken from the roast we had had the night before.

"You were out again?" Sophie asked.

"Yes," I said, unwinding my scarf once more. When I went to stuff my gloves into my pockets, my fingers brushed against cold metal. I took out the key and set it on the table, where Brianna promptly picked it up to examine it.

"Where'd you find this?" she asked.

"Miss Zenobia's office," I said. "Although I think it would be more accurate to say it found me."

"What have you been doing?" Sophie asked.

"I had to figure out what was going on. I keep feeling like I'm being attacked. Bludgeoned over the head, cut across the throat, stabbed a dozen times. It's not pleasant."

"What's been happening now?" Brianna asked, looking up from the key.

"I've been attacked. I told you before," I said.

"That's not what you said before," Brianna said. "You said 'episode.' Then you said you didn't actually sense any danger."

"Well, I thought it might just have been some strange sort of headache, only it happened again and again," I said. "You were busy, so I went over myself to investigate."

"And?" Sophie prompted.

"And I found a dead body," I said.

"Again?" Sophie groaned.

"And Nick found me inside the apartment that was supposed to be locked with the dead body," I said. "Also, it had only been dead for less than a minute, so."

"So now we're going to have to dance around another police investigation?" Sophie said.

"No," I said quickly. "Nick is handling it."

"We can't keep dealing with this level of attention," Sophie said. "If people get suspicious, if they start watching us closely, it's going to be very hard for us to maintain the bridge."

"They won't understand what we're doing," Brianna said. "There will be rumors. Probably pretty horrifying ones. People like to tell all manner of evil stories about the supposed doings of witches. It's not going to matter that none of it is true."

"But we can't ignore this stuff either," I said. "It's magic. The police can't handle it."

"Are you sure this isn't something going on with you medically? Or maybe induced by your own magic?" Sophie asked.

"Interesting," Brianna said. "Your attempt at the illusion spell appeared to be blocked. Blocking that flow of energy, where would it have gone? It's possible... I need my books," Brianna said, shoving toast into her mouth even as she got up from the table.

"It was magic, and it wasn't me," I said, catching her arm before she could dash away. "The body in the wardrobe, it wasn't there when I opened the door. Then suddenly he was there. He just popped into existence before my very eyes. And I can't say for sure, but he was dressed like he belonged in 1927."

Sophie and Brianna exchanged a quick look. Then Sophie pushed back from the table and went through the solarium and out the back door with a bang.

"My detectors should have gone off," Brianna said with a frown.

"I'm not sure this involved the time bridge," I said. "I went into the world of webs, and I looked at everything. The wardrobe seemed magical, but not like the crystal ball."

"Not evil?" Brianna asked.

"Yes, but also not as powerful. The glow wasn't as strong. Still, this body appeared out of nowhere, inside a magical object. What does that mean?"

Brianna frowned. "I'm not sure," she admitted at last. "I need to do more research."

"I did everything I could think of to do," I said. "I didn't see a connection with the bridge, and I didn't sense the presence of Juno."

"No," Brianna agreed. "There is more magic in the world than you might think. It's not all connected with us. You might just have gotten caught up in something."

"Someone else's story," I said.

The back door banged against the side of the house, and I suspected the wind had torn it out of Sophie's grasp. It was that sort of night.

She came back into the kitchen, hair standing on end in all directions, her cheeks and the tips of her ears bright red.

"You should've taken a hat," I said.

"There is nothing wrong with the time bridge," she said.

"No, I would have detected it," Brianna said.

"I wanted to be sure," Sophie said. "Nothing has changed. Our wards stand as sure as ever."

"So what does this mean?" I asked.

"It means this is none of our business," Sophie all but snapped. "If Nick is taking the heat for you, let him."

"But the police can't solve this," I said.

"Then they don't solve it," Sophie said. "If you're right and this happened ninety years ago, then it's either already been solved, or it's been a cold case so long it's reached, like, absolute zero."

Brianna opened her mouth. I suspected she had something to add about absolute zero, but from the look that Sophie shot her, she snapped her mouth back shut and turned her attention back to her toast.

"What if I get attacked again?" I asked.

"I told you before, just stay out of the building next door," Sophie said. "We all had to give up things for magic. I guess that's yours."

My throat was too thick to squeeze out words, so I just nodded and headed up the back stairs to my room.

But just staying away from Nick's apartment wasn't going to help. I had been attacked here, in my own room. Perhaps being in his apartment, walking past that door, was what had started all this, but now that it had started, I seemed powerless to stop it.

I could have said that to her. It was all true, after all.

But I didn't. Not because I didn't think she'd listen to me. I knew she would.

But it didn't matter. Because it was suddenly clear to me that as much as she had been putting a good face on it, she was hurting.

She had left someone behind in New Orleans, and she was missing him more than she would ever let Brianna or me know. She was missing him terribly. And me, spending time with Nick, whether that was a date or some not-a-date gray zone thing, whatever, it was hurting her.

She had teased me and encouraged me by turns. She had even taken me shopping largely with an eye to what I could wear when I was out with Nick. I was putting together a lot of random comments now, and it was all perfectly clear.

She was hurting, and I couldn't fix it. I could only do what I could not to make it worse. If that meant less time with Nick, or just less time openly being seen coming and going from places with Nick, so be it.

But letting this little mystery go?

Not even.

CHAPTER 7

*L*ong, slow breath in. Long, slow breath out. Long, slow breath in.

I narrowed my focus to just the air filling my lungs like I was supposed to.

The air filling my lungs had an earthy smell to it. It was strong enough to be distracting.

I usually did this meditation outside, in the garden, but not when it was this cold. But even in full autumn, with the leaves drifting down all around me, the air had not had such a thick smell of growing things and decomposing things to it.

The solarium was full of potted herbs and little plants. I think Mr. Trevor harvested some of them to use in his cooking. Usually, when I would sit at the table in the solarium to drink coffee and look at the morning paper, I didn't really notice the smell. Now, sitting on my meditation mat in the middle of the floor, I couldn't seem to tune it out.

But I had to. I was supposed to not be thinking. Not any thoughts at all, and smelling the earth was giving too many thoughts.

I refocused. Deep breath in. Deep breath out.

I managed a few more cycles of breath, but a sudden cracking of noise made me jump. It sounded a bit like an old steamboat had crashed into the basement with crunches of metal and hisses of escaped vapor.

But I knew what it was. It was the heater. The heater wasn't as old as the house, which had fireplaces in every room for a reason, but it couldn't be a whole lot younger. It was a great monstrous thing that kicked on with a tremendous amount of noise, like gears grinding, like some metallic thing about to breathe its last breath and then die.

So, another thing I had to tune out. But I knew that after a minute or two, the worst of the noise would quiet down to just a blast of air running through vents.

Deep breath in.

Ugh. The first blast from the heating vent had that burned smell, and sitting on the floor as I was, the vent was at my level and just behind me. The first time you fire up a house's heater in the fall always smells like burnt dust, of course, no matter where you live. But in this house, it was like every day was the first day of fall when you ran the heater and cooked everything dwelling in the ducts. That smell.

Okay, focus. Deep breath in (ignore the smell). Deep breath out.

Suddenly, just as I was getting into the groove of it, sunlight hit me full on the face, so bright it turned my eyelids deep red.

The southern sun, much lower in the sky than when I had first started meditating here, had found a gap between the shrubs and a little narrow pathway between the clusters of plants that lined all the glass walls.

With a sigh, I shifted my position to turn my back to the sun.

Not a bad idea, actually. Aside from getting the light out of my eyes, the warmth of it on the back of my neck was soothing. I closed my eyes, determined now to truly tune out the world around me.

I focused on my breath, the feeling of my chest rising and falling, the feeling of the air moving through the passageways of my nose and throat.

I wondered if the police had figured out that that body was from 1927?

Ugh, thoughts again. Still, what had they figured out? I knew it was early yet, only about six in the morning, but I also knew that Nick was an early riser. If he knew anything important about the police investigation, surely he would've called me.

I was curious if they had figured out anything about the wardrobe. I was certain it was a magical artifact, but I had no idea what the magic was. Was it the sort of thing only I could perceive? Or did it have larger effects that anyone could perceive?

The crystal ball that Mina Fox had owned had done both kinds of things. It had an energy only we witches could feel, but it had spoken with a voice all could hear, and shaken the walls of the Fox house and far more. But it had been very obvious to me from the moment I looked at the web of its threads that it was a deeply magical item with its own agenda.

The wardrobe had seemed rather benign. No intent, no traces of sentience. But I didn't know what that meant.

Was Nick going to call me? Or was I going to have to call him?

Was the reason he had not called me yet because he was arrested as a suspect? Did they think he had something to do with it because he was there in the apartment?

What if they had arrested him for breaking and entering?

My eyes flew open. My heart was pounding, and there was no getting back into a deep meditative state now.

I told myself I was being silly. There'd be no reason for them to arrest Nick. He lived next door, his story was completely plausible, and he'd probably called his friend Nelson Fisher, a detective with the police force. Nelson knew Nick was trustworthy. And besides, there'd be no evidence against him.

Still, why hadn't he called?

Of course, I could always call him. But my phone was upstairs. And it was, after all, just after six in the morning.

I took a few deep breaths and resettled myself on my mat. I could at least wait until eight to call him. Eight in the morning was a normal person time of day to be up and about. In the meantime, I had work to do.

I settled back to just an awareness of my breath. This time I was so focused I didn't even notice when the heat stopped running. I only had a vague sense of the hot air that had been blowing across my knees dying away.

I focused on my breath for an immeasurable amount of time, but then I had an idea. I went a little deeper, shifting my consciousness like I'd done in the hallway outside of the apartment door. I moved myself outside of my body, but this time I stayed close to it.

I looked at the glowing threads that joined into a pattern of tangles and knots to form my body. I observed all the threads, how they interacted with each other but also how they interconnected with the form of myself that I was in this place. I couldn't actually see myself in this place, but I could see threads that interacted with me.

I looked more closely and observed which threads glowed with my heartbeat, and which threads flanked it but were growing dimmer. I was sure those represented my lungs, not currently working. I reached into my own chest and snagged some of those dim threads. Then I tweaked them, giving them a little tug.

I saw the chest part of the body in front of me rising and falling with even breaths, timed to how I was pulling on those threads.

I had figured it out. I could keep an attachment to my body even as I ranged away from it.

Well, I wasn't sure. It seemed to be true, but if I trusted it and was wrong, I'd be dead.

I should stay close to my body, pay attention to it more often than I had back in the apartment building. I couldn't get distracted, couldn't wander off for longer than I could hold my breath.

So I stayed near my body, hovering over it, but I shifted my awareness to the larger world around me.

I expanded my awareness further out from my body inside the solarium, spreading out throughout the house. I sensed Brianna already working in the library. Then I expanded further and felt Sophie going through the motions of her wand work in the attic. Then I expanded further until I was aware of the world outside the walls of the house. I sensed Mr. Trevor just coming up the front walk with his arms full of groceries.

I contracted back until I was once more aware of the body in front of me, my own body. It was still breathing evenly, just as I'd intended it to.

So far, so good. Now to expand a bit further.

I shifted my focus, expanding ever wider. But just making a larger sphere of perception was going to be too tiring, I was sure. So instead, I shifted it sideways, centering on the building next door.

I was no longer aware of Brianna or Sophie or Mr. Trevor. All I knew of inside the school was the single thread of awareness attached to my own body.

But mostly, I was focused on Nick. Was he in the building next door?

If I lost my focus for even a moment, the world of webs would fall into a pattern of chaos. I could not make heads or tails of it. I had to really focus, to see the things as they appeared in the real world. This was easier to do with living things like people than it was with the walls of the building. Its threads were so cold and unmoving I could scarcely see them.

I wasn't sure how exactly I was going to find the correct apartment when the walls and floors were so vaguely defined to me. But then I saw the brighter pattern of a person. The pattern felt familiar. Orderly, calm, kind.

Nick's grandfather.

And in case I wasn't sure, I looked at a different, smaller pattern nearby, at his feet, a more chaotic pattern of energy. Finnegan. He appeared to be waiting for something to fall to the floor.

I guessed that Nick's grandfather was making his breakfast, something with bits that Finnegan liked. Probably something with cheese.

But there was no sign of Nick. I moved my awareness through the building, always paying just a little bit of attention to the thread connecting me to my own body, to feel the slight tug that meant it was still breathing. But there was no sign of Nick.

Behind his grandfather and Finnegan, I found a space that

contained whispers of his presence, like a ghost he had left behind. I guessed that I was perceiving the room that he slept in. He had left little bits of himself and his personal energy behind, but he wasn't there now.

Did that mean he had been arrested after all? Or had he gone in to answer questions and was still at the police station?

That nagging worry was starting to snowball on me, and I knew that real panic would throw me out of this meditative state. Instead, I focused back on Nick's grandfather, the calm and orderly energy that was the pattern of his threads.

That was comforting, but not just because of the kindness that it radiated. It told me that Nick's grandfather wasn't worried about anything in particular. And if Nick had been out all night and never come home, I didn't think that would be true.

Perhaps Nick had just gone to class. I had no idea what time he started classes, or if he went in early to get a run in or workout in the gym before the first class started. It sounded like the sort of thing he would do. I knew he was still very early to rise and early to bed, an artifact from his time in the military.

In the end, I had to make the conscious decision not to worry about that anymore. Which sounds easier than it was. But I did it.

Finally, I moved my consciousness into the empty apartment next door. That energy was familiar; I had been there before. Not just physically, I had perceived its web pattern of threads before. It was like coming back to a very familiar place.

The body was gone. That I was sure of. Even though the body was no longer living, I would still have seen remnants of its former living shape in the world of threads more clearly than I perceived walls. But it was gone.

And so was the wardrobe. I wasn't sure what that meant. I know the police take things from the scene of a crime, to process as evidence, but the wardrobe seemed awfully large for that.

I felt the thread in my hand, the attachment to my body, still tugging at my awareness with each breath. My body was doing okay. I took one last moment to pass my awareness over the empty apartment rooms.

Why was I attacked when I had passed in the hallway? How was this related to the body, which didn't even appear until hours later when I was attacked for the third time? And how had it attacked me the second time, when I wasn't even in the building?

Maybe attack wasn't the right word for what happened to me. After all, I hadn't been physically harmed myself. It was more like I was aware of something happening to someone else.

So does that mean three people had been attacked? Three people, and only one body to show for it?

I started to wonder what had been going on inside that wardrobe before I found it. Maybe bodies had been winking in and out of existence the entire time, and I hadn't realized until I opened the wardrobe door.

Still, why me? Was it because I passed too close?

Or was this something to do with my magic being the rare kind of time magic?

I could ask Brianna, but I didn't think she would know any more about it than I did.

Suddenly I was back in my body, eyes open, pushing myself off up onto my feet before I even realized that I'd made a plan. I slipped out the back door, shivering almost at once. I had come downstairs to meditate dressed in yoga pants and a tank top. Clothes nowhere near warm enough for this kind of weather.

Plus, I had no shoes on. But I would only be outside for a moment. I went out to the orchard and stood amidst the trees. This was always where I could sense the time bridge, the one that permanently connected our world to 1927.

It was getting easier and easier to switch to the perception of the world as a web of living threads. This time it happened almost instantly, and my body was still on its feet. I looked up at the bridge spiraling over me.

It never ceased to be awe-inspiring, not just in concept, but in execution. So few could perceive it, but it was a thing of great beauty, all shimmering with inner light, at once a piece of architecture and a living thing. But I forced myself to look not at the whole of it, but at every single part, combing over it with all the care and attention that I could muster, examining every orderly thread that made up its matrix.

Sophie was right. I saw nothing out of order. And I knew that Brianna trusted her own detection equipment completely, and none of them had raised an alarm. Still, I felt more reassured having seen it with my own eyes. Whatever was going on with that wardrobe, it had nothing to do with our time bridge.

Now there was just one more thing I wanted to do.

"Juno?" I called. I waited a moment, awareness moving over the structure as I looked for any sign that Juno had heard me.

I called her name three more times. Each time, there was no sign of anything changing. I could still sense her presence there, but she was such an integral part of the bridge itself. The threads that made up who she was as a person were thoroughly intermixed with the threads of the structure itself. I couldn't really grasp one part of it to direct my calls to. None of it was more or less her than any other part.

I knew she heard me, but she was ignoring me. And that was annoying because if there was one person who could explain to me what all this meant, it was the one person who shared my special power.

But clearly, she wasn't interested in talking to me.

I was on my own.

CHAPTER 8

The moment I came back into the house and felt the heat on my skin, I started shaking all over. Nope, definitely not dressed warmly enough.

Still, I couldn't stop shaking. It was excessive, and I don't think it was just from the cold. All the shifting of my awareness back and forth from the web world was more exhausting than I expected.

I had left a hoodie on the chair in the solarium before I had started meditating. I quickly pulled that on before going into the kitchen.

I heard the voices and identified each separately. I knew they were all in there, my fellow witches as well as the steward of the estate, Mr. Trevor. But the look of alarm when they all saw me standing in the doorway was a bit more extreme than I had expected. Sophie and Brianna, waiting for the coffee machine to finish dripping, gaped at me in open-mouthed shock. Mr. Trevor had just loaded up the refrigerator with his purchases and froze in the act of folding the paper grocery bag to store with the others in the cupboard in the butler's pantry.

"Miss Amanda, are you quite all right?" he asked me.

"Yes, I'm fine," I said. But I was very aware that my hands were still shaking. I shoved them deep into the pockets of my hoodie.

Sophie raised a single eyebrow. Brianna's eyes narrowed as she studied my face. I wasn't fooling anybody.

"Perhaps this will help," Mr. Trevor said, setting a Styrofoam container on the kitchen counter. "It was a bit of an impulse buy for me, especially as I wasn't even sure if you were awake yet and these really are best when they're hot. But I thought you might like these."

If there was ever a concept and a person that completely failed to fit together in my mind, it was "impulse buy" and "Mr. Trevor."

He opened the catch on the box with the squeak of Styrofoam on Styrofoam, then flipped the lid back to release a cloud of steam. The smell hit me: egg and cheese and bacon all on fresh-baked English muffins.

"Oh, that smells perfect," I said. Sophie quickly handed me one, and I ate half of it in one enormous bite.

"Sometimes my instincts are good," Mr. Trevor said, clearly pleased. He took one sandwich for himself, wrapped it in a cloth napkin, and, giving us his usual little nod that felt like a bow, he disappeared up the back stairs to his personal office.

I wondered just what it was he did all day. Besides, hone his psychic powers to be attuned to knowing in advance just what I was hungry for.

"You were in the backyard?" Brianna asked.

"Briefly," I said. "I wanted to take a look at the time bridge. Not that I didn't believe you," I quickly said to Sophie.

Sophie waved the remark away with a hurried gesture. "No, we should all back each other up, right? And Amanda, I'm sorry about the things I said last night. I didn't really mean–"

"No need to apologize," I quickly said. "You weren't entirely wrong, were you? I do need to start doing more on my own. I can't keep expecting the two of you to do all the heavy lifting for me. No, you weren't wrong."

"I wasn't kind, either," Sophie said.

I couldn't answer right away, as I had stuffed the rest of the sandwich into my mouth. It was so good, the heat of it quickly calming the last of my shivers that had come from the cold. I could feel it refueling me after the magical strain as well. The effect was instantaneous.

The warmth of the food warming my body, and that delicious mix of fat and protein and carbs flooding my bloodstream...

Okay, technically, I was only just starting to digest it. None of it could possibly be in my bloodstream that fast. But you know what I mean. Sometimes food just feels that way.

When I was feeling more myself, I plunged into what I really wanted to say. "I have some things I wanted to talk to you to about," I said to the two of them. "I was just working on my meditation practice when I thought of a way that I could make sure that my body is still breathing, even when my consciousness is away from it. I'm not sure what people that do that astral projection thing do, but when I'm in that place, I can see the threads that connect all things. I see my body like a web of energy all interconnected, but I can also focus on the threads that are individual parts of my physical form. So I just had to grab a couple of them that corresponded to my lungs and make sure I stayed in contact with my body with those threads. My heart takes care of itself, thank goodness."

"That sounds like the same sort of thing I've been reading about," Brianna said.

"Well, all I know is, it worked. I was careful. I checked back on myself a lot, but I managed to leave my body. Three separate times."

"That sounds really risky," Sophie said. "I thought you were going to wait for someone to watch while you attempted this?"

"I was, but it just sort of flowed out of that meditation practice," I said. "I wasn't really thinking about trying to do it; I just tried to do it. There was no plan. But it worked."

"Still, I want you to promise you won't do that again. Not that exact thing, of course. If you say it's safe, then I'll believe you that it's safe. But don't try another risky thing without letting one or the other of us know what you're up to."

"We do the same with each other, Sophie and I, when we try new things," Brianna said.

"While, mostly Brianna," Sophie said. "She's the daredevil."

"Fine," I agreed readily, reaching for another sandwich. "But that's not all that I wanted to talk to you about."

"Okay, so go ahead," Sophie said. The coffee machine had finally finished running, and she filled three mugs and carried them over to the table. Brianna brought the rest of the Styrofoam container, and she and Sophie took a sandwich each as they waited for me to talk.

"Some of this I told you last night, but just let me say it all again in order. I'm still trying to get it all straight in my head."

The two of them nodded, picking at their sandwiches, but didn't interrupt.

"So it all started last night," I began, "in the hallway outside of that empty apartment building. I was just walking by the door when I felt the sudden splitting pain in my head. At the time, I wasn't sure what it was. It could've just been a really intense headache. I've never had a migraine, but I imagine that anything that could be described as a thunderclap headache would be pretty close to what I was feeling right at that moment. But I didn't know what it was, or what it meant.

"That was the only one that happened before I saw the two of you. So, like I said, I wasn't sure what it was. But then, when I had gone to my room to go to bed, it happened again. Only this time, it wasn't a headache. It was a burning pain across my throat, as if someone had just slit my throat with a knife. It was very intense, but like before, it ended very quickly. That was harder to chalk up to natural causes. Headaches people get all the time, but a pain like that across the outside of your throat? It just didn't seem natural.

"So I decided to go back to the apartment, to see if I could find out more about what was going on. I still didn't really have any kind of a theory, except for that it seemed to have started outside the apartment, so perhaps the apartment was part of it. So, like I told you, I found that key and went next door and used it to get into the apartment.

"There was nothing in it but dust and cobwebs and an old wardrobe in the bedroom. It was dark—the lights didn't work—but when I opened the wardrobe door, I know I was looking inside an empty wardrobe for at least a part of the second. But then I was attacked again. This time it was like being stabbed all over my body, first in the chest and then in my back. And when I opened my eyes, there was a body, and it had been stabbed all over, just where I had felt the pain the moment before. And the body was from a different time period."

"But we don't know that for sure," Sophie said. "There could be other explanations."

"I suppose so if one wanted to keep an open mind about all possibilities," I said. "But I don't think that kind of openness is going to do us much good. Because we know that there are ways to connect our time to that time. And even though we've all looked and we're sure that our bridge wasn't part of it, that doesn't change that basic fact. If we see the body of a man dressed for 1927, it's not exactly improbable that he's from 1927. We know that there are ways to move through time, and we also know that the bridge here is not the only one."

I waited for the two of them to respond. Sophie was nodding thoughtfully, but Brianna was just staring down at the top of the table, a mouthful of food that she seemed to have forgotten to finish chewing puffing out her cheeks.

"The wardrobe isn't over there anymore. The police moved it. I wanted to get another look at it, but it's gone," I said.

"But you said you looked at it pretty closely last night, right?" Sophie asked.

"Yes, I did. I didn't notice anything in particular about it. It seemed like it might be magical, but it was nothing like Mina Fox's crystal ball. Nothing like that at all."

"Well, it wouldn't be," Brianna said, realized she was talking with her mouth full, and quickly chewed and swallowed before going on. "The crystal ball contained Mina Fox. That is a very rare particular kind of magic. I wished we'd've gotten a chance to look at that wardrobe. I would like to do some tests on it as well. There are lots of ways of crafting magical objects that don't involve such malignant energies."

"But we're surrounded with that kind of stuff," Sophie said. "This house is full of it. Maybe a good next step for Amanda would be to be spending more time in that other place. What did you call it? The web world?"

"Web world works," I agreed. "And that's not a bad idea."

"No, I think it's a very good idea," Brianna said. "In fact, it would make sense to look at some specific items first. Miss Zenobia created lots of things with the specific purpose of containing magical things she didn't want to get loose. If you examined enough objects enchanted with such spells, you'd know them again if you saw them."

"That's a good idea," I said. "But there was something else I was stewing over," I said. "I was thinking about why was I was feeling these things all."

"Because you were closest?" Sophie suggested.

"But that second time, I wasn't. I wasn't even in the building. So, did it mark me with the first one and follow me here? Or was it something else?"

"You have a theory," Brianna said.

"Yes, I have a theory," I said. "Because that man, I'm sure he was from 1927. He moved across time, not using our bridge, but somehow he moved across time."

"And time is your sort of magic?" Sophie asked.

"Exactly," I said. "What if that's why it happened to me? Maybe I'm more attuned to disturbances in the space-time continuum or whatever. Or what if it was my power that attracted the sensations to me?"

"Interesting," Brianna said. "Actually, I've read about something not too different from that."

"Really?" I asked.

"Yes, I don't know about time magic in particular," Brianna said. "There are other kinds of magic certain witches have more of an affinity to. The most common are those having an affinity for a particular element. Like fire or water or earth. And the attraction with objects connected to that same element, that's actually pretty common. Some witches have it worse than others, of course. It depends on your raw power and your capacity for control both. But I'm thinking of one fire witch in particular. She was one of the ones who had no training until she was an adult. Her mother died or something. But she was a fire witch without knowing it, and she attracted fire like nobody's business."

"That doesn't sound good," Sophie said.

"It wasn't," Brianna said. "Every house she lived in as a girl burned down within a year or two of her moving into it. It was pretty tragic. I mean, she didn't even know she was a witch. At least not the first couple of times."

"Then what happened?" I asked.

"Some other witches found her and took her in. And then she studied. She studied her power, and magic in general, and she learned how to control the attraction."

"Sounds like something I need to work on," I said. "I don't want this sort of thing to keep happening."

"Or to intensify," Sophie added. I nodded.

"Well, I can see if I can find that book," Brianna said. "Also, I could ask the witches that raised me. They know other witches, lots of other witches. One of them must've had experience with this. Like I said, the elemental kind of magic is pretty common."

"I would appreciate that," I said.

"And I need to find you some of those magical objects," Brianna said, already fishing her little notebook out of her pocket. She turned to a blank page and started making a new list. With lots of bullet points.

"Really, there's no hurry," I said. "When you have the time. I have some things to work on in the meantime myself."

She gave me an absent-minded nod but kept on writing out her list.

I took one more egg sandwich and carried it up the stairs with me to the library. But I didn't go back to the little corner table where all those books were still waiting for me. Instead, I went to another little windowless alcove, the one where we kept our computer.

After a few moments working my search engine magic, I had a name to go with the address for the apartment next door to Nick's grandfather.

Mr. and Mrs. Lambeau.

Only a last name, no first name. And further searching didn't turn anything else up. But then, Nick's grandfather had said that they kept to themselves.

Still, I wasn't sure how much use I would get out of knowing just the last name.

I looked at the clock in the corner of the computer screen and saw that it was a couple of minutes after eight. A perfectly reasonable time to be calling someone.

But when I called Nick's cell phone, it went straight to voicemail. I disconnected and sent him a quick text.

Nick, hope all is well. Any updates?

I waited, probably for too long, but he never answered. I supposed he was in class and had to keep his phone put away.

Still, I couldn't wait around all day. I had to find something useful to do.

I supposed if I searched online resources long enough, I could find a list of everyone that was reported murdered or missing in November 1927. I even knew where I'd start such a search.

Or I could just go to 1927 and check the local papers there myself. Yes, that was the much more appealing option.

CHAPTER 9

As much as she talked about it, Brianna had never quite gotten around to building a weather prediction machine. Well, not really predicting, just telling us what things were like on the other side of the bridge in 1927.

Still, that's what almanacs were for. I quickly checked and saw that while the temperature was largely the same, they'd had some recent snow. So boots would be in order.

I was cautious going up the attic steps in case I disturbed Sophie, but she had gone on to some other activity, and the room was quite empty. Without her warm wind, it was chilly and dark in the space under the slanted roof. I scurried over to my closet and assembled an outfit as quickly as I could, remembering to include hat and gloves, boots and a coat. Then I went back to my much warmer room to change.

Dressed and wearing Cynthia's little amulet tucked under the neckline of my burgundy day dress and with the golden skeleton key in one pocket, I went downstairs and out the back door.

The thin wool of the coat wasn't as wind resistant as more modern fabrics, but it was warm enough. I was still feeling a little shaky from all the work I had done that morning, so I conserved my energy and just let the amulet carry me across time.

I would feel guilty later about missing the opportunity to practice what was really the key spell of my calling.

Then I was once more in the backyard, but a version of our backyard with shorter trees, different garden features, and a fresh layer of snow covering everything. It was lovely, but almost too bright under the full light of the morning sun. I scurried up the steps and into the solarium. There, I took off my hat and coat and slipped out of my snow-covered boots. There was a row of warm slippers standing near the back door. I didn't know whose were whose—I didn't even know who was around in 1927—so I just chose a pair at random and slipped my stockinged feet inside.

The heater that kept the house warm might've been newer in 1927, but it wasn't any more effective. The house was filled with the same slightly chill air as it had in my day.

I passed through the kitchen and up the front steps to the library. As always, it looked like I had just missed everyone. Books sat on tables with the pages open, notebooks covered in writing beside them, pencils resting as if they'd just been set down. There were plates of toast with a few bites missing, and they didn't look the least bit stale. Even the cups of tea that rested nearby were still steaming.

The table closest to the door, under the windows that opened out onto the porch that stood over the front door, was where Mr. Trevor always put the newspapers in the morning. But he hadn't started that tradition; it was already how they did things in 1927. I pulled a chair over to the table, sat down, and paged through every newspaper from cover to cover, scanning every story for the slightest hint of anyone being murdered or any prominent person that was missing.

Nothing. Nothing at all.

It was possible that the man I saw wasn't anyone important enough to be reported in the newspaper. I hadn't gotten a good look at his clothes, not in the dim light that came through that narrow window. Especially not in the shadows inside the wardrobe. I'd only gotten a good look at his hat.

It had seemed like a very nice hat, nicely made and stiffly new. I was sure that he must have been someone important. So why wasn't he in the paper?

Was it possible that the wardrobe didn't follow the same timeline as our bridge? In that case, he might've died weeks or months ago.

He might not even be dead yet.

If only Nick could get back to me with details. The police had the body, but I doubted they would get an ID, as helpful as having a name would be. But perhaps he could get me a photograph? Something I could carry around in 1927 and ask people if the man looked familiar?

Having gone through every newspaper, I went to the shelf in the library where we kept all the local directories, one for each year as far back as the school had existed. In my day, this shelf was overflowing. In 1927, there was still lots of room. I started with the most recent directory, then went back one by one for at least ten years. There was no sign of any family named Lambeau living anywhere in St. Paul.

They might've been recluses, or they might have kept themselves out of the directory for some other reason, nefarious or not. But if they were as wealthy as Nick's grandfather had implied, they should be listed. As a prominent family, it wasn't really optional.

Which left the possibility that they just weren't in St. Paul yet. That made sense. They couldn't have moved into the condo until the late 1980s. I guess I had just assumed that they'd moved in there from some other part of St. Paul. But they could be from anywhere.

I ran a hand through my hair in frustration. They could be from anywhere; the body could come from any time. I wasn't really narrowing anything down.

I went back downstairs, slipped my feet out of the warm slippers and back into the boots. I buttoned up the coat and pulled the hat down low over my ears. The gloves were very thin and not very warm, but my coat had pockets deep enough to keep me warm up past my wrists. I plunged my hands in those pockets because I wasn't intending just to go back to the present. I was going to take a walk around 1927.

Or rather, I wanted to take a walk around the web world of 1927.

I went out to the end of the back porch and looked up at the house next door to Miss Zenobia Weekes' Charm School for Exceptional Young Ladies. In my day, this was a condo built in the 1980s. It had been something else in the years between, I knew. But right now, it was the house that belonged to Coco and her family. At some point, it was going to burn down. I'd never looked up exactly when. I kind of didn't want to know. Brianna said we couldn't change things that had happened in the past and was very insistent that we never, ever try.

The house that was built to follow, I knew, hadn't lasted very long either. But that wasn't fire. It hadn't been built well in the first place and was torn down by new owners to build the condos.

There would be no reason at all for the wardrobe to have existed on that plot of land through so many different buildings and owners, but I just had to be sure. I sat down on the end of the porch, making sure to keep the wool of my coat underneath me so I wouldn't get too cold.

Then I closed my eyes and shifted my awareness to that other place.

This time, it happened in the blink of an eye. It was getting easier and easier. I looked down at my body, then caught hold of the threads to keep my lungs functioning.

Now inside the web world, I looked up at the building next door. It was perfectly ordinary, in truth, but with more little knots of thread that I knew meant living people than I expected. I'd never been inside of it. I'd only ever met Coco outside in her yard and the rest of her family, not at all. But given the time period and the wealth of the family, I would guess they had a lot of servants.

There wasn't any sign of the wardrobe. There wasn't any sign of anything magical at all. It was what I had expected to see, and yet still I found it vaguely disappointing.

I came back to where I had left my body, the thread still pulsating gently in my non-corporeal hand as my body kept breathing. Then I looked up at the house looming over me. Miss Zenobia Weekes' Charm School for Exceptional Young Ladies. In my time, it looked perfectly ordinary, if a bit overly filled with not-so-ordinary things.

There was something wrong with what I was looking at now. I couldn't see exactly what it was, but something was telling me that there was something just a bit off. What was it?

I looked at it closely, as a whole, and then following the paths of the individual threads. They formed walls with a bit more life to them than other buildings had. I could see the brighter thready knots where magical objects stood, largely in Miss Zenobia's office, but some in the library and others scattered about.

Exactly the same as I was used to seeing. So what was different?

I looked more closely at the threads, how they interacted with the world around the house. No, that was still perfectly ordinary.

Then, all at once, I saw what was different. None of the threads were touching me.

That was strange. I shouldn't be able to perceive something that wasn't interacting with me, not when I was in the real world. And yet I had, every time I came to 1927.

Or had I? Was this another strange side effect from my magical power being one related to time? Was it only me that was not interacting with the house?

No, I was sure that wasn't true. Well, maybe not sure. I'd have to have Brianna and Sophie come back to 1927 with me while I looked at them from inside the web world, but I was pretty sure. This was some other magic, some magic in the house itself that only worked on people that were not in the correct time.

This must be how it was that we never ran into any of the other students, although it always seemed like they had just been there. We never heard their voices, so it wasn't like they were fleeing the room before we came in, and yet they always had left so suddenly that things remained behind. Sweaters on the backs of chairs, the sandwiches, and tea that were almost but not quite consumed.

While that was a horrid thought, that every time I went into the room that I thought was unoccupied, it was actually filled with people that I couldn't quite perceive. And I suppose they couldn't quite perceive me either, but there was no denying the fact that when I sat down in a chair that still had someone's sweater across the back of it, I was probably sitting right down on top of someone, overlapping in the space over the chair's seat with that person. We would be existing in the exact same space, but at not quite the same time.

Well, I couldn't wait to tell Brianna about that. She would want to come back to test herself, just as I did, but I could easily imagine how excited she would be at the idea. She would want to do experiment after experiment.

I turned my attention away from the house, back to the bridge that joined this time to my own. I examined it closely, but just like on the other end, nothing was unusual or out of place. I would occasionally see a thread running through it that I knew belonged to Juno, but never enough together to say that she was truly there. I called her name, a couple of times, but I wasn't exactly surprised when she didn't bother to answer.

She was biding her time for something. I didn't think she was sulking. That wouldn't be like her.

At some point, she was going to make yourself known again. And that would probably spell trouble for me. It was probably best that she kept to herself for now.

At any rate, I was certain this wardrobe business had nothing to do with her or with the time bridge. As much as I would appreciate being able to talk to her about my power, there were a lot of downsides to talking to her as well. She with her silver tongue and her hidden agendas. No, I was better off handling this alone.

Not that I was handling it so well. I was getting absolutely no clues. I had a name, but I wasn't even sure if it was a useful one. If the Lambeau family had been gone from the apartment for so long and taken all the other furniture with them, they might not even own the wardrobe at all. Someone else might've stuck it there, for any sort of reason, knowing that the family would never come back to see it there.

That apartment room, it felt so familiar. After having been in it just one time, I had been drawn back to it pretty easily. It had sort of called to me like I'd slid downhill towards it with very little effort.

Would the wardrobe be just as familiar? If I just brushed past it mentally while expanding my awareness, would it draw my focus to it?

Well, it was worth a try.

I checked my body, saw that it was still breathing as evenly and regularly as before. A thought drifted through my mind, just wondering if my body was getting truly cold from sitting on the concrete for so long. But this would only take a minute.

I expanded my awareness, going past the charm school with its strange, not-quite-there behavior, sweeping past Coco's house with its mundane details, then moving to the other houses on the other sides as well as front and back, an ever-expanding circle that widened around me, brushing through millions and millions of tiny threads, all interacting with each other. None of them had quite the familiar feel of the wardrobe that I was looking for.

It felt so easy when I was doing it, just expanding out, wider and wider, but then all at once, it seemed like it was just too many threads. I was examining each of them individually, but they were acting on me collectively. There was no sign of the wardrobe, and now my consciousness had expanded so far out with all those threads pulling at me that I wasn't sure I could get back down to my body again.

I forced myself not to panic, to do something like take a deep breath, even though in this alternate reality I didn't actually breathe. I concentrated on the throbbing of the threads I held in my hand, the breathing of the body I had left behind.

That helped. That was my focus. I came back into my own body within two breaths, and I was indeed deeply cold to the bone. But when I tried to get up my legs were like rubber, and I fell to the snow.

That was strange. I tried to get up again, but my legs still didn't quite want to take my weight. On the third try, leveraging myself off the edge of the patio, I managed to get onto my feet.

Once, back in the early days of my weight training, I had overdone it just a little bit on leg day. That had felt something like this.

Only this? Was all over my body, not just my leg muscles.

I was shaking, worse than I had after the magic I had done that morning. Now I knew just shifting my awareness around had been draining me dry, but a little too late. These things came at a price. It was gonna take more than three fried egg sandwiches to bring myself back up to normal. Five or six might not even be enough to do it.

Luckily, I had brought the amulet with me. I held it now, closing my eyes, more out of weariness than any desire to shift my consciousness around.

When I opened them, I was in the backyard in my own time. The wind was whipping around me, pulling at my hair, but the ground was that ugly brown color that comes in late November when one really wishes it would just snow already.

And standing in front of me, deep concern in his eyes, was Nick.

CHAPTER 10

For whatever reason, seeing him standing there staring at me made me shake even harder, and I was already shaking pretty intensely. I hugged my arms close around myself, hoping he would write it off as just me being cold.

But the look on his face wasn't a gentle worry I might be uncomfortable. It was something more intense than that.

Oh my goodness, had he just watched me appear out of nowhere? There's a huge difference between someone telling you they are a witch, and believing what they told you, and actually seeing them do something incredibly magical right in front of your eyes.

But it wasn't shock and surprise on his face, either. He looked really freaked out.

"What is it?" I asked.

Nick didn't answer, just reached into his pocket and pulled out a handkerchief.

A handkerchief. An actual handkerchief. I would expect his grandfather to have one of those in his pocket at any moment, but not someone my age.

Then he touched the handkerchief to my face just under my nose, a very gentle touch, and only when he had pulled the handkerchief away to refold it and bring it back to my face did I notice it was covered with blood.

"Oh," I said, reaching up to touch my nose, but he gently brushed my hand away to dab at my face again. "I had no idea. It must be the dry air."

He still didn't speak, but the look he gave me was deeply skeptical.

"I'm cold," I said, only partly because I was sure he could feel my whole body shaking. "Let's go inside."

"Let's," he said. He helped me up the steps and through the door into the solarium. I stopped there to slide off the boots and take off my hat, gloves, and coat.

Again, when I looked up at Nick, there was a strange expression on his face. I looked down to see what he was looking at and realized that I was, of course, still dressed in the 1927 dress. It wasn't quite the sort of thing that a trendy hipster girl would wear. Too everyday functional, not pretty enough.

And even if it were, he knew me well enough to know I was not a trendy hipster girl.

"I need tea," I said. "I really am quite cold. Would you like some tea?"

"Tea," he said with a little nod.

I went into the kitchen, and he followed me at a slower pace, the bloody handkerchief still in his hand. I put the electric kettle on and busied myself with cups and tea bags.

"I like Earl Grey at this time of day," I said, avoiding his eyes. "But I still have English breakfast, if you prefer. Or something herbal maybe?"

"I'll have what you're having," he said. He leaned on the counter that ran between us, his eyes still on my dress.

"I texted you earlier," I said, pulling out tea bags and dispersing them between mugs.

"And called," he said.

"Yes. I haven't been able to find any useful information about that wardrobe or the man inside of it. But I didn't have much to work with. I was hoping you knew more."

"I know some things," he said.

"Great," I said.

There was a long, awkward moment while we waited for the water to come to a boil. Then I filled both the teacups and carried them over the kitchen table. He handed me the handkerchief, and I pressed it to my face, seeing that my nose was bleeding once again. "Dry air," I said again.

"There's more going on here than dry air," Nick said.

"Of course there is," I said. I waited for him to ask another question. Was he just curious about my out of time period dress, or had he actually seen me stepping out of nowhere in the backyard? Did he have some theory as to why my nose was bleeding that wasn't because of dry air? Had he learned something about the body or the wardrobe that was making him so suspicious?

"So, what did you have to tell me?" I finally asked, when he offered no questions of his own.

"Well, it's an antique," he said.

"It looked like one," I said.

"We have to get an appraiser to tell for sure, but one of the other officers at the police station thought it looked like a genuine Louis XV."

"I don't know what that means," I said. "I'm guessing expensive?"

"From France, during that time when the palace at Versailles was the big thing. So yeah, old but in good shape. Worth a lot of money. That, or it's just a pretty good knockoff. It's hard to say. But Nelson managed to track down the family. Well, not really a family, just an old couple who never had children. They used to live here, just like my grandfather said they did, but they've been living in a gated community in Mexico for the last few decades."

"Gated community in Mexico?" I asked.

"Yeah, I guess it's something rich people do, move to Mexico but live in a walled-off community of only people from places just like where you're from. That way, you don't have to bother learning any Spanish."

"That sounds odd," I said. "Why would you live in Mexico if you didn't want to be around any Mexicans?"

"Climate?" Nick offered.

"You can get the same climate in New Mexico or Arizona," I said.

"Tax dodge?" Nick added, but then he shrugged. "I'm not sure it's important."

"I guess not. Did they say anything about where they got the wardrobe or why they left it behind when they took the rest of the furniture?"

"They got the wardrobe at an estate sale in New York City in the 1970s," Nick said. "But they didn't have any paperwork on it, didn't really remember any details, and they'd never had it appraised. They must've suspected it was genuine, but they didn't bring it with them to Mexico."

"I don't suppose you got to talk to them at all?" I asked. He shook his head no. "Pity. I'm curious whether the thing gave them the creeps or something. Like maybe they thought it was haunted. Did anyone ask why they left it behind?"

"As best as we could tell, it just seemed like they forgot it here. Is that a magic thing? Like someone didn't want the wardrobe to be moved, so the Lambeaus just forgot it existed?"

"I don't really know," I admitted. "I'm still really new on all the stuff. I think I told you before I moved here, I didn't know that any of us were even real. It's only been a few weeks. I'm still trying to catch up."

"Is there anything, in particular, you need me to find out about that wardrobe?" he asked.

"Are they gonna put it back in the apartment? In case I need to take another look at it or something?"

"I don't know," Nick said. "Once it gets taken out of evidence, it will be up to the family what happens to it. If they don't want it moved to Mexico, they'll probably just sell it. If you wanted to let them know that you are interested in purchasing it, I could pass that information along."

"Yes, do that," I said. Not that my monthly allowance was enough to buy genuine antique furniture from the palace of Versailles. But I was pretty sure there was a household budget for such things when they were magical. I would have to ask Mr. Trevor.

"So anyway, from the point of view of the police investigation, the wardrobe was pretty normal. Especially compared to the man's body," Nick said.

"I didn't get a real close look at him," I said. "I didn't realize how few details I had taken in until I was trying to investigate him further. I couldn't see his clothes very well in the dark. Did he appear to be wealthy, or working class, or something else?"

"Well, his clothes are strange," Nick said.

"From the 1920s, yes," I said. "I noticed his hat."

Nick made a noncommittal sound; his attention focused on bobbing his tea bag up and down in his tea mug. I took a sip of my own tea, still too hot. Then Nick gave me a sidelong look, taking in the burgundy dress I was wearing.

"His clothes rather match yours; I would say," Nick said.

"Yes, about that—" but he didn't let me go on.

"That wasn't the only thing odd about him, though. I doubt they'll find a match for his dental records. The medical examiner joked that his dentist was probably doing it as a sideline to his barbershop business. He had several missing teeth. Others had abscesses that had been filled, but the amalgam was like nothing the ME had ever seen. And apparently he had had his appendix removed, but the surgical scar and x-rays looked so brutal that the medical examiner wondered if the man attempted to do it himself."

"Could they remove appendixes in the 1920s?" I asked. I wasn't that up on the history of medicine.

"Apparently, yes," Nick said. "Because I asked. The medical examiner was wondering if perhaps this man had been to some really remote part of the world. Like really, really remote. Third World country wouldn't be remote enough for this kind of surgery. That's when I asked if it was consistent with something that might've been performed in the 1920s."

"What did he say?" I asked.

"I think he thought I was joking," Nick said with a sigh. "Or, maybe not exactly making a joke but taking something serious that wasn't meant to be serious. Like asking him what doctors could do in the world of Star Trek, or in the world of Games of Thrones, serious geek stuff like that. So he took it seriously, like a hypothetical, and said yes, what he saw would be consistent with the sort of surgery that might be performed in the 1920s. Different techniques, not so elegant, but they did have anesthesia then. And they did do appendectomies. But Nelson just looked at me like I was insane. I don't think he's bringing me with the next time he goes to talk to the ME."

He took a long drink from his tea mug, set it down on the table with the slight clink of ceramic against the tabletop, then looked at me. "So, are you going to explain about your clothes?"

"I can," I said slowly. "If you want me to. If you really want to know. But think carefully before you say yes. You can't unhear anything I tell you."

Nick looked at his hands for a minute, then looked at me again, not at my dress this time, but straight into my eyes. "Yes."

"So there is a reason why I was brought here," I said. "Like I told you, I didn't know anything about any of this until I came here just a few months ago, the day I met you. Not even then, really. It wasn't until the next night that it was all explained to me. Sophie, Brianna and I were all brought here for a reason. The two of them, they knew they were witches. They had been practicing their magic for years. But it was a complete surprise to me. And it's more than just being a witch. We have to be here for a very specific reason. We need to use our magic to protect a very specific thing."

"And this has something to do with 1927?" he asked.

"Yes, it has everything to do with 1927. I don't know how or why, but the old witch that lived here before we came here, the one who died and left us this place, she created a sort of portal through time.

You wouldn't be able to see it; I don't think you'd even be able to sense it. I couldn't even for a long time, and technically I'm a witch. But there is a bridge in the backyard that connects this place to the exact same house, only in 1927. And when I couldn't find out anything about the wardrobe or the man that disappeared from here, I went back to 1927 to have a look around. Of course, going back in time, I have to dress to fit in. So."

Nick didn't say anything for a long time. I didn't want to rush him, and I was willing to answer any question that I could if only he would ask.

At last, he drained the last of his tea, set the mug down with another clink, and got up from the table.

"Nick?" I asked.

"I think I better start digging into some really old case files," he said. "Research. But it will probably draw less attention than actually asking these crazy-sounding questions of the medical examiner."

"Yes, I'm sure that's true," I said.

"Here, I made copies of the photos of the body and the wardrobe," he said, digging into the pocket of his coat. "The body is a bit gruesome, but the face came through all right. If anyone knows him, I think they will find him recognizable."

"Thanks, this is really helpful," I said. "If I find out who he is, I'll let you know. You can decide what to do with that information yourself."

He nodded again and headed out the hall towards the front door, but stopped with his hand on the knob to look back at me again.

"Amanda?" he asked.

"Yes?"

"That pain you had in your head? Outside the apartment door when we were walking to my place for dinner? Has that been happening again?"

"Not since we found that dead body," I hedged.

"So that's just a thing that was happening because of the wardrobe and the dead body?" he asked.

"I assume so," I said. "I kind of think that at some point we might turn up other dead bodies. One with a bashed head and one with the slit throat."

He gave me a look like he was desperately hoping I was joking, but knew that I wasn't.

"Just be safe," he said to me.

"I will," I said.

He gave one more nod, then left.

CHAPTER 11

The tea had helped a bit, but I was still shaky. I poured myself another cup, helped myself to a double handful of smoked almonds from a jar in the cupboard, and several cubes of sharp cheddar cheese from the fridge. By the time that was all gone, I felt recovered enough to walk up the stairs to the library.

I was a bit worried about interrupting Brianna again, but she seemed to have been waiting for me. The minute I stepped into the room, she jumped up from her table and ran over to me.

"I have so much to tell you," she said.

"I have a lot to tell you, too," I said.

"You first," Brianna said, folding her arms as she waited.

"I went back to 1927," I said. "Remember how I told you it's getting easier for me to shift my consciousness to the world where I see the webs?" Brianna nodded, her eyes watching me intently. "Well, I did that again, but over there."

"Did you find the wardrobe?" she asked.

"No, but I was just talking to Nick downstairs. Apparently, the family didn't buy it until the 1970s, and they bought it in Manhattan. It doesn't seem likely that it was even in the area here in 1927. But I didn't know that at the time, so I did try to look for it."

"And?"

"And I didn't find it, but I saw something else. While I was over there, I shifted my attention to look at the house itself. This house, Miss Zenobia Weekes' Charm School for Exceptional Young Ladies."

"Does it look different there than it does here?" Brianna asked.

"Slightly," I said. "I'd like to take a look at it again when we're all over there. I want to see what it looks like with you there, but not today. What I did there, on top of what I already did this morning, I think it was too much."

"You do look really drained," Brianna said. "But about the house?"

"The house," I said. "The house looks normal in most respects, except for it doesn't interact with me at all. It's like it's closed itself off to me. I can see it, smell it, everything as usual, but I'm not quite inter-acting with it in the same reality."

"A protective spell?" Brianna asked. "That's why we can't see the students who were there in 1927, even though we know that they're there. Or Miss Zenobia or Cynthia or anybody."

"That was my thought as well," I said. "We should do some more experiments with that."

"Experiments, definitely," Brianna said. "But you don't think this is related to either the dead body or the wardrobe or the attacks?"

"No, I don't think so. So if you're saying that the experiments can wait, I'm inclined to agree with you."

"I've been busy while you've been away," Brianna said. "I've been in contact with my mentor from back in Boston."

"Someone from your mother's coven?" I asked.

"No, not from the coven," Brianna said. "This was a witch I found myself when I was a student at the university. It took a bit of work; she doesn't like interacting with others anymore. I'm not even really sure how old she is, possibly even older than Miss Zenobia. She talks about Boston in the old days, and I swear she speaks like she's been there since the 1600s. But she was my mentor in the magical part of my studies when I was there. I haven't been in contact with her as much as I should've been since I came here. I've been so busy. Busy, but not keeping up with my studies. But she answered my call right away. She's available any time, she said. I'm wondering if you can do a drawing of some sort to show her what that antique wardrobe looks like?"

"I can do better," I said, digging the photograph out of my pocket.

"Perfect," Brianna said, clutching the photograph tightly. "I'll call her back up so I can show her this."

"Call her up and show her?" I repeated as she raced to the computer alcove.

"Sephora doesn't like to interact with strangers, but that doesn't make her a technophobe," Brianna said. "I talk to her all the time through video chat. She prefers it to conventional phone calls. She likes to make eye contact. It's a thing."

"Well, at the moment, it's a pretty handy thing," I said.

The wait screen flickered and was replaced by the image of an older woman. Her steel gray hair was pulled back into an untidy bun, and she was wearing a truly astounding amount of tinkling jewelry. Nothing fancy, nothing expensive, just a lot of it. Her fingers were covered with rings, the bangles on her wrists jangled even as she was moving her hand back from answering the computer call, and I wasn't sure how anyone could wear so many necklaces without being bowed over with the weight.

"Brianna, lovely to see you," Sephora said.

"Miss Sephora Marlowe, may I introduce you to my colleague, Miss Amanda Clarke?" Brianna said formally. "And Amanda, this is Miss Marlowe."

"Call me Sephora, dear," she said with a jangling wave of her hand.

"Pleased to meet you, Miss Sephora," I said.

"As I mentioned before, we're calling about an object that we think has been enchanted. We're not sure if it's something with a long history or a more recent enchantment. The wardrobe in question is an antique."

"What does it look like?" she asked, leaning closer into her computer camera.

Brianna held up the picture, holding it steady in front of the camera lens as Sephora gazed at it intently. "Ah yes. Unless I'm very much mistaken, which I rarely am, I do know what that is," she said. "Very interesting piece."

"What is it?" I asked.

"The wardrobe this puts me in mind of was one of a pair. As furniture, they both date back to the time of Louis XV of France, but they weren't enchanted until the 1880s. They were identical and owned by a pair of sisters. The Rousseau sisters. Identical twins, actually. They used to perform parlor magic as a bit of a lark. They had been from a very wealthy family, but France being what it was at the time, they lost their estates and all the wealth with it. The lark became their only source of income. They were supporting themselves with these little magic shows, but they were really quite good. Of course, everyone they performed for thought they were just illusions. The Rousseau sisters would make objects move from one wardrobe to the other."

"A fairly simple spell, especially if both wardrobes were on the same stage," Brianna said.

"Quite correct," Sephora said. "But they had wonderful chemistry with each other and were a joy to watch, apparently. You can find stories about them in mundane accounts of the day if you look. But nothing lasts forever, especially not youth. Not even if you're a witch. In later years, when their popularity started waning, they modified the act, which meant modifying the spells. Frankly, they had someone else modify the spell for them. Their skill was more in stage presence than actual magic, and it would've been a very complicated spell," she said.

"What sort of spell?" I asked.

"Well, if the stories are to be believed, it was a sort of time magic. They would put things in one wardrobe. Both wardrobes would be visibly empty for a certain period of time, then they would open one, and there the object would be. Alas, it did not help the popularity. It was too slow of an illusion, not enough of a show even when they started using people instead of objects. Of course, that's not what really destroyed the two of them."

"Destroyed?" Brianna repeated.

"It's an unhappy tale with an unhappy ending," Sephora said. "By the time they started dabbling with time magic—or rather as I've said, had someone else dabble in it for them—they were beginning to look like women in the last of their middle years and were not so lovely in their provocative parlor show outfits as they used to be.

"Then tragedy struck in the form of man, a recent widower, that both sisters fell in love with at the same time. The man chose one sister, marrying her and taking her with him to Manhattan, and one of the wardrobes with them. The other sister never married. She stayed in Paris until her dying days, and her wardrobe was always with her."

"How sad," I said. "They were witches. You'd think they'd be more sensible."

"You don't know the half of it," Sephora said grimly. "The man in question wasn't worthy of either of them. The marriage lasted less than a year after they arrived in Manhattan. He was a philanderer, and no witch would take that betrayal lying down. She left him, but she never went back to Paris and her waiting sister. So far as I know, her wardrobe always stayed in Manhattan. But she died with no children, and no one knows exactly what became of her wardrobe."

"And the other wardrobe?" Brianna asked.

"The other wardrobe was passed down to a niece when that sister died. But it was destroyed in a house fire," Sephora said.

"Do you know when that happened?" Brianna asked.

"Let me check," Sephora said. I expected her to swivel in her chair, to pick up one of the large tomes I could see stacked high all around her or filling the overstuffed bookshelves behind her. But instead, she turned her attention to another computer. There was a tapping of keys, and she leaned forward to squint at the other screen before turning back to us.

"Late October 1927," she said. "It was a house in Paris. And yes, it says here just what I told you, that no one knows what became of the other wardrobe. Perhaps it also was destroyed. Although apparently not," she said, pointing with her chin towards the photograph sitting next to Brianna's hand.

"If it disappeared in New York, that makes sense," I said. "This wardrobe was purchased in New York in the 1970s."

"That gives more than seventy years of not having its whereabouts pinned down precisely," Sephora said.

"I think that other date, October 1927, that's the more important one," Brianna said, tapping her fingertips to her bottom lip.

"Because of your time bridge?" Sephora asked. I gave Brianna a sharp look. I thought the time bridge was our secret. Did that exclude other witches?

"The wardrobe didn't move through the time bridge," Brianna said. "But the bridge has a very strong influence on things around it. Even if we can't see it, other things feel its pull. Isn't that true?" she asked her mentor.

"I would assume so," Sephora said. "But you know, time magic, it's a rare gift. And those who understand it, they are often recluses. They don't teach their magic to outsiders, and they don't write things down."

"So you don't know anyone who knows anything about time magic?" I asked.

"Amanda has shown skill in time magic," Brianna hastily added, apparently worried her mentor would think that I was being rude.

"No, I do not," Sephora said with a thoughtful air. I appreciated that while her brain was constantly running at a dizzying speed, she seemed better capable than Brianna of having a one-on-one conversation at the same time. Perhaps that came with age. "I can put word around, but I'm not sure it will turn anything up. I haven't heard of a witch with that sort of power since I was a very young girl. It's very rare."

"If you find anyone, please let them know I'm looking for them," I said. "It's very difficult, having a sort of magic no one can teach you how to use."

Sephora gave me a hard look, her eyes drilling deeply into mine. I wanted to look away, but I was certain that that would be the wrong thing to do. I held myself steady, and let her finish her assessment.

At last, she gave a sharp nod—to me or to Brianna I couldn't tell—

then wrote something down on a pad near her elbow. "Like I said, I'll put the word around. But no promises."

"Thank you, thank you very much," I said sincerely.

"Yes, thank you, Sephora," Brianna said.

"If you ever need anything, just give me a call," Sephora said. "You know I don't like to travel, too many people in too small of transports, But I can answer questions over the phone anytime. It's no problem at all."

"I'll remember," Brianna said, then gave a little wave before terminating the call. "What now?" she asked me.

"Now, I guess I go back to 1927," I said. "It's just as well I never changed back into my normal clothes."

"What are you going to do in 1927?" Brianna asked. "It seems pretty clear that the wardrobe wasn't there."

"Unless it was," I said. "It's just too weird a coincidence that the other wardrobe was destroyed just before all this started happening."

"Well…" Brianna said, clearly wanting to argue the timelines. I knew what I meant. She knew what I meant. But she wanted to argue the minutia, and I knew she would quickly turn my mind into a pretzel if I let her get going.

"Also, I've got this," I said, showing her the picture of the man who had died. "No one here knows who he is. The usual methods of getting an ID aren't going to match anything. I really think he's from 1927. So if I show his picture around in 1927, I might find someone who recognizes him."

"Unless he really was from New York," Brianna said.

"Well, there's just one way to find out," I said. Then I went back down the stairs, grabbed my coat, and went back through the backyard, back to 1927.

CHAPTER 12

The sun was just setting as I went into the backyard. The wind was finally starting to die down, but the deep cold was getting ever deeper. And the brownness of so many dormant plants waiting to be blanketed in snow was just as depressing as ever.

Then I stepped across the bridge and found myself surrounded with dazzling snow. The sun was just as low in the sky, but the icy crystals were amplifying it all around me.

I didn't bother going into the house; I had nothing to learn there this time. Instead, I went out on Summit Avenue and walked a block over to Maiden Lane, where Edward had his little garret over one of the garages. I'd never been inside, only about halfway up the steps, but I remembered which one it was along the row of similar garages.

I carefully picked my way up the snow-covered stairs, knocked on the door, then knocked again.

Clearly, he wasn't home. I hadn't planned for that at all. But there was no light through the tiny window next to the door, no sign of footsteps in the snow on the stairs save mine. So he must've left before the snowfall and hadn't been back yet.

I wondered where he was. When had it snowed? It had looked fresh when I came through in the morning, so I supposed it was possible that it was snowing when he went to work, stopped after he got there, and he wasn't home yet.

I didn't know where his office was, but I knew one other place that he could be. I walked back to the charm school, then on next door to the house, the one Coco's family lived in.

Coco's older sister, Ivy, was the object of all Edward's affections. The first time I'd met him, he'd been coming down the porch stairs after trying to pay a call on her the day after meeting her at a dance. Every time since then that I'd run into him, he pretty much had either been coming or going from seeing Ivy.

I looked up at the warm lights glowing through the windows. They looked so homey. Nobody in that house knew me but Coco, and she was thirteen. I couldn't very well knock on the door and pretend to be calling on either a guest who seemed frequently less than welcome or on the youngest member of the household.

So I stayed on the sidewalk, empty in the cold of impending nightfall. I closed my eyes and expanded my awareness to pass over all parts of the house.

It was crowded with even more people than before, and I suspected that they were having a dinner party. Most of the glowing clusters of threads were in what I would assume to be the dining room, a few others in the kitchen around the back of the house.

But none of the patterns of glowing threads felt like Edward. I'd never looked at Edward while in the web world, but I was pretty sure if I encountered him I would know him. I would recognize his very nature in that pattern.

He wasn't there.

So I guessed he really was still working. That seemed plausible, though. I knew he was hoping to get a promotion, hoping to earn more money and impress Ivy's father. That must be what was happening.

But it left me with no one to help me find anyone who might recognize the man in the photo I had in my coat pocket.

Well, there was one other person.

I walked past the cathedral into St. Paul itself and then down to the riverfront. I'd gone this way before, more than once, but I had never gone alone, and never this close to nightfall. The sun was just barely in the sky, and it was getting darker by the minute, especially as the buildings grew taller around me.

Then I turned down the street on which I found the former beer hall, still some sort of public house that was never not filled with rollicking men. It was no longer actually a functioning beer hall, not during prohibition, but I found it hard to believe that no one there was doing any drinking. Not from the loudness of their voices and the redness of the cheeks. And sober men seldom went into back alleys to settle disputes with a fistfight. All that spoke of some sort of alcohol, and probably not anything as benign as beer.

Alas, that fistfight was going on in the alley I needed to pass through to get to the cellar stairs. I gathered my coat more closely around me and slipped behind the crowd of jeering onlookers, staying close to the wall. This kept me as far from the fight as possible, but all too close to the very strong stench of urine against the stones of the wall. Apparently, the beer hall had no bathroom. I was very grateful I was wearing boots.

The voices of the crowd shrieked as one of the combatants knocked the other down to the ground. He rushed forward and was going to start kicking the other man before he could get back on his feet, but the first man's friends gathered around and broke up the fight. He didn't seem willing to stop kicking, not even when offered a jug of something frothy. There was a loud commotion, with lots of coarse language, but no one was looking my way.

I went down the steps and through the cellar door, having to duck under the beam at the top of the frame to get into the cellar.

The urine stench of the alley gave way to the stale smell of the beer-soaked timbers overhead. Years and years since the sale of beer had been declared illegal, and still, the smell just wouldn't go away.

I saw a light shining from the far end of the cellar, at the bottom of the sloped floor, This space was blocked off by a wall of crates so that I couldn't quite see where the light was coming from, but that was where Otto kept his office.

I could hear voices talking and laughing together. None of them seemed to be Otto's, but I had noticed that compared to his minions he tended to be quieter, more soft-spoken.

I clutched the photo more tightly inside my pocket, then realized I was wrinkling it and pulled my hands out of my pockets. I knew Otto well enough, but his underlings always made me nervous. If they were here without him, I'd have to come back later.

I walked down the slope to the gap in the wall of crates, stopping just where the shadows ended, not quite in the light of the single bulb beyond.

None of the men were familiar. And they were older than his usual crew and burlier. They looked less like nimble thieves in the gray area between juvenile delinquents and hardened criminals and more like longshoremen.

I lingered in the gap between the crates, staying in the shadow as my eyes scanned the room for any sign of Otto or anyone I recognized as being an acquaintance of Otto's.

No one. And the usual assortment of stolen merchandise and crate after crate of booze was missing. Something had changed here, and I didn't know what it meant. But I wasn't going to stay and ask. I would wait for Edward. Edward would know where to find Otto.

But I had lingered too long. Just as I started to turn away, one of them called out. "Hey, missy," he said. "What are you doing down here?"

"Someone lurking in the doorway?" another asked, moving closer to get a look at me. "Step into the light so we can see you."

I was disinclined to take that action. The one who had spoken first was standing behind the table that had been Otto's desk. Perhaps he was their leader. He certainly looked the oldest, a few wisps of color-less hair all he had to comb over his sun-damaged scalp.

The one leering at me, reaching a hand out as if in some caricature of a gentleman about to help a lady out of her carriage, was younger. He must work around boilers or something else that gave off incred-ible heat, to judge from the layers of burn scars over his bare forearms and the overwhelming stench of sweat he carried with him like a cloak.

"I was looking for Otto, but I can see is not here," I said.

For some reason, they all found this very funny.

"Looking for Otto?" the first one laughed. "Do as Len says and come closer into the light so we can see you."

"No, I'd rather not," I said.

I can see you," Len said. While I'd been looking at the first one, Len had drawn even closer to me, and he was leaning into the shadows to peer up at me. I glared back at him, but I don't think he was intimidated. "Otto has nice taste, eh, Kev?" he said. "He's very popular with the young ladies, our Otto."

"Otto isn't here. This is our place now. But anything you need Otto for, you can get from us," Kev said.

His tone had changed dramatically from low-level threat to smarmy salesman. I didn't know exactly what he was offering me, but I was pretty sure I didn't want it.

"It's a personal matter," I said. I suddenly realized that I was speaking more and more primly by the minute. Rather, like when Sophie was starting to get stressed and she would punch up the Creole in her accent.

I hadn't realized I did that. Interesting.

"We handle personal matters too," Kev said.

I realized too late that I had lost sight of at least two more of them. Kev and Len hadn't been alone when I came down, but they looked alone now.

Then I heard a rustling behind me and found myself trapped in the narrowing opening in the wall of crates, Kev and Len in front of me, and two more men behind me.

"I'm a student at the Miss Zenobia Weekes' Charm School for Exceptional Young Ladies," I said, putting on an even more prim tone. "Perhaps you've heard of it? Perhaps you are acquainted with the specific skills of the students?"

"Miss Who's Charm School for What-Now?" Kev said, and all four of them started laughing. "No, not familiar, although I'm a big fan of special skills," he said.

He left no mystery as to what he considered those to be, but it was really beneath me to show offense at so obvious an insult. "Well, that does make things difficult," I said instead. My hands wanted to shake terribly. I squeezed them into fists close at my sides, hoping they wouldn't notice.

"You really must come forward and step into the light," Kev said. I could tell his patience with this game was wearing thin.

The two men behind me were standing very close behind me. I could smell the whiskey on their breath. They had used it to wash down bad meat and old cheese, to judge from the smell, and they were competing with Len for most intense unwashed body smell in a goon lurking in a cellar under a beer hall.

"No, I think it's time for me to go," I said.

"Well, we can't just let you go," Kev said. "We don't know who you are. You could be some kind of snoop. Maybe even from the government, eh?"

The others seemed to find this uproariously funny. I clenched my fists tighter at my sides. Then my right hand brushed up against the wand that I kept inside a special pocket inside my coat. Slowly, I unbuttoned my coat, to the predictable amusement of the men around me.

Then I pulled out my wand to brandish it at all of them.

Kev's eyes got wide, but not in fear or even surprise, unless that look was the surprise of humor. He started laughing even harder. He was laughing so hard I was worried that he would choke.

But then Len reached out with one meaty hand and caught my arm, gripping my wrist with a crushing intensity.

The bones were grinding together. I could feel them approaching the breaking point.

But he was grabbing my left hand, and my wand was in my right.

Not that I thought a spell would save me. But I didn't necessarily need to do anything magical with it for it to be a weapon. Instead, I gripped it tightly and jabbed it as hard as I could into his overall-covered stomach.

He fell back, turning darkly red in his anger, swearing words that I never had even heard before.

But that quickly changed to silence, a silence that made my ears ache. It was like his rising anger was jacking up the air pressure around us all. He looked like a bull getting ready to charge.

I didn't have much time.

I tried to back away, to run, but the two men behind me closed ranks. There was no way for me to get around them. And if they grabbed me, I knew I was done for. Now that I had made Len angry, there was no going back.

There was only one thing left for me to do. I closed my eye and summoned up my vision of fireworks, the one I had tried to conjure the day before. It hadn't worked then, but I hadn't been this scared then. And hadn't Brianna said the fear for one's life was a huge amplifier of nascent magic?

Well, I could only hope she was right about that. But if adrenaline was energy I could burn, I had plenty of it to spare.

I raised my wand. My eyes were still closed, but I remembered where each of them had been standing. I pointed my wand at Len and let everything that had been building up inside of me channel through the wand and out into the room.

I couldn't tell if it did anything at all. Was it just dying sparks like before?

No, because suddenly everyone was screaming. Wild screams of real terror, not screams of laughter this time.

I opened my eyes.

I had been picturing fireworks, a sort of sparkly display that might be impressive. Surely any show of magic would be usable as a threat.

What I had gotten was more like the fiery breath of a dragon firing out of the end of my wand. Len had fallen back until he collided with Kev, the two men together backing away, throwing up their arms against the searing heat.

Searing heat. I could feel that. I was conjuring more than just light;

I was conjuring heat. Not a physical object out of nothing, but not bad.

I felt hands brushing the back of my coat, attempting to grasp handfuls of it, and I spun to train the dragon breath on the two men behind me. They fell back, scrambling out of the way, and I couldn't blame them. The light and the heat were both very convincing.

But I only had a moment before they discovered that nothing was actually burning. Not the clothes they were slapping at, not their bodies, not even the crates of very old wood filled with alcohol that were scattered all around us. And once they knew that my spell was an illusion, they would be closing in on me with a great deal of anger.

Still, there was a little part of me that was very, very eager to get back to Brianna, to tell her all about it. My spell, my spell had really worked.

But in order to tell Brianna, I had to get out of there alive.

I tucked the wand away and ran up the cellar steps, back out to the alley beyond.

And promptly collided with yet another body.

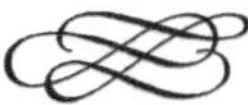

$\mathcal{I}$ pushed away from hands that tried to grasp me, flinging my coat back to once more bring my wand up at the ready.

But the hands hadn't been trying to pin me. They had only been trying to steady me. And the owner of the hands, a familiar-looking boy of maybe twelve, raised them both as if in surrender when he saw my wand.

"I'm so sorry! I wasn't looking where I was going!" he pleaded.

"Don't I know you?" I asked. Some of the onlookers from the previous fistfight were still standing together at the end of the alley, and a few were looking our way, but I didn't put my wand away. Let them think whatever they liked.

"I'm Benny. I drive for Mr. Mayer," he said, hands still up in the air. "And you're Miss Clarke. I drove you to that crazy lady's house."

"Yes!" I said, recognizing him at last. He looked like he'd grown a foot since I'd seen him last.

Then I heard footsteps coming up the cellar floor behind me. Footsteps and angry voices.

"Benny, I need to get out of here in a hurry," I said.

"This way," he said, leading me past the fistfight crowd to the wider street beyond. I saw Otto's shiny new car parked next to the curb on the far side of the beer hall.

"Otto is still here?" I asked.

"No, miss," Benny said, bending to pick up one of two crates that stood on the corner under the streetlight. "But I can take you to him. I'm going there right now, just as soon as I get these loaded up."

I looked back down the alley. Kev and Len were just emerging from the cellar, but we were looking up and down the alley without seeing me standing on the far side of the gathered men.

But that wouldn't last long.

I put away my wand and bent to pick up the last of the crates.

"Miss!" Benny protested. "You can wait in the car. I've got this."

"Hurry, Benny," I said from between gritted teeth. The boy was stronger than he looked, or he had taken the lighter of the two boxes.

Or I was out of shape. But let's pretend it was one of the first two.

Benny set the crate on the ground while he struggled with opening the trunk. I set mine down on top of his, then quickly climbed into the back seat, scrunching down low in the seat.

I took my wand back out. Not that I suddenly knew any more spells or thought I could get away with the same trick twice. I just felt better with it in my hand.

Benny loaded both of the crates in the back and shut the lid with a bang. I expected him to get into the driver's seat, but he didn't.

Then I heard Kev's voice. "About this high? Wearing a navy blue coat and hat? Really chaotic hair? Carrying a wand?" Each question had a rising inflection, like he was losing patience, and I guessed Benny was giving him a lot of blank looks.

"Carrying a wand? I would have remembered that!" Benny laughed. His laugh ended with a woof of air being driven out of his body, and the car lurched as he impacted with it.

"Answer my question, kid," Kev said.

"I did," Benny said, gasping for the breath to form words. "I didn't see no dame. This isn't the place for dames. Not dressed like the one you described for sure."

Someone else spoke, the words too low for me to hear, but the tone urgent.

I heard Benny's feet hit the pavement as Kev let him go. A moment later, the driver's door opened, and Benny slipped into the car.

"All right, miss?" he asked, adjusting the collar of his shirt.

"Me? I'm fine," I said. "Did they hurt you?"

"No, miss," he said. Then he started the engine.

I stayed low in my seat until we were several blocks away. By the time I sat up, we were nowhere near the riverfront. We were among the newer, taller buildings of St. Paul's growing downtown area.

"Otto lives here?" I asked.

"Lives? I have no idea where he lives," Benny said. "But he works up here now. He's got some nice digs. You'll like it."

"He certainly couldn't have found worse ones," I said, but not loud enough for Benny to hear. Benny's feelings for Otto went beyond loyalty. They were closer to the domain of hero worship.

Benny pulled up to a curb and braked the car much more smoothly than he had done the last time I was his passenger. "Never mind the crates," he said when he opened the door to help me out. "I'll get some of the fellas to help me with those. I'll take you straight to Otto."

"Wait, Benny," I said, catching his sleeve before he could start down the sidewalk. "What are you going to tell Otto about what just happened?"

"Everything," Benny said, as if that were the only possible answer.

"I shouldn't have been down there alone," I said. "I'm not saying those men were right to try to do what they tried to do, but part of the blame is on me."

"I can leave out your bit," Benny said grudgingly. "But they manhandled me. I'm Mr. Otto's squire. No one can manhandle me like that and think they can get away with it. I have to tell that bit."

"Very well," I agreed. But I was pretty sure the minute Benny told his tale, whether I was still standing there next to him or not, Otto would put it together. I doubted those guys would have been harassing Benny if not for my account.

Benny led me to one of the tall office buildings, then through a narrow door just around the corner from the main street, a smaller door into a private business.

The business turned out to be a diner. It looked like it was being squeezed by whatever businesses rented space on either side of it. There was barely room for a narrow counter with stools in front of the kitchen down one side and a single line of cramped booths down the other.

The smell is best not lingered on. The smell of rancid grease was so thick in the air I could feel it clinging to my hair just as I was passing through.

I mean, I worked in a diner for half my life. I know what a diner should smell like. It wasn't this.

"Come on," Benny said, taking my hand when I lingered in the doorway. He led me past all the booths to another door in the back. It was a cheap wooden door painted the same off-putting green as the walls, and I had taken it for a broom closet until Benny knocked on it.

"Password," a voice said, and I saw a single eye peering out of a peephole I hadn't seen a moment before.

"Swordfish," Benny said.

The peephole slammed shut, and once shut it blended perfectly with the rest of the door. Undetectable.

Then the door swung open. I could hear voices talking together in low tones, the soft tinkle of someone jostling the cymbal on a drum-kit, a soulful woman's voice singing warmup exercises.

"This is the Greasy Spoon," Benny said.

"That's a terrible name," I said as I followed him inside, through a space that had clearly been designed to hold brooms, then through a hole cut in the back wall of that closet and down a flight of steps to a very different sort of cellar than the one Otto had dwelled in before. Some rich family might have stored their wine down here once.

"He's changing it," Benny said to me as we stepped into the first circle of golden light pouring down from an art déco lampshade above. "To Sophie's."

We came down the last few steps, and I saw a tiny stage on the other side of the cellar where a band was laughing and chatting together while they set up their equipment. The singer looked vaguely familiar. I didn't know much about 1920s music, but I was sure I had seen her photograph in a book or magazine.

Around the stage were a couple dozen of intimate little tables with tall chairs clustered around them. They were pulled back enough from the foot of the stage to allow for a little dancing, but I had a feeling most of the patrons were coming for the contents of the endless array of bottles behind the gleaming bar on my left.

"Sophie would like that," I said, and I was pretty sure it was true.

Benny grinned at me, then became all business again, leading me past the bar to another door designed to blend in with the dark paneling around it.

Benny knocked briskly, then stepped back, arms folded.

"Enter," said a voice from within.

"That means you," Benny said, opening the door for me and giving me a little wink as he guided me inside, then shut the door behind me.

The door was thicker than it looked. The moment it fell shut, all sounds of the club behind me were cut off.

Otto was sitting behind an imposingly large desk, the headset of a shining phone in his hand. He smiled at me, then pointed to one of the chairs in front of his desk. Then, as if called back to a continuing conversation, he started talking loudly into the phone.

And really, he didn't have to whisper to keep his conversation private. My two years of high school Spanish were going to be no help deciphering his rapid-pace German.

I sat on the very edge of one of the two leather chairs and clasped my hands together in my lap. Otto, still speaking into the phone, pushed a bowl of nuts closer to me and gave me an inviting gesture, but just shrugged when I shook my head no.

I know I speak no German, but I was certain that when he hung up the phone, the conversation hadn't quite been over. It was too abrupt. But then he was turning his attention onto me.

"So, how's Sophie?" he asked, folding his hands over his stomach as he leaned back in his chair.

"She's fine," I said. "Benny tells me you're going to name this club after her."

"Benny talks too much," Otto said sourly.

"I hope I didn't get him into any trouble by mentioning it," I said. "He did rather save me earlier this evening."

"Save you?" Otto said with a frown.

"I was lost, and he brought me to you," I said. "I needed to see you."

"Without Edward?" Otto said, as if that fact had deep significance.

"I couldn't find Edward, actually," I said, digging in my coat pocket for the photographs. "I just need a moment of your time. I'm wondering if either of these mean anything to you?"

I set down the photograph of the wardrobe first. Otto picked it up with his fingertips, careful not to smudge the image, and examined it carefully before setting it back down with a shrug.

"Well, that was a long shot," I said, then handed him the other photograph.

Otto knew him at once. He didn't speak, and his face didn't change in the slightest. I was sure he was a first-class poker player. But I knew. There was the spark of recognition in his eyes.

"You do know him," I said.

"Yes," Otto admitted, his face still betraying nothing. "Tell me, why does he appear to be dead in this photograph? Is this some sort of trick?"

"No trick," I said. "He looks dead because he is dead."

"Since when?" Otto asked.

"Since last night," I said. "Maybe sooner."

"Oh no," Otto said. "Not sooner. Not even last night. That's not possible."

"How do you know?" I asked.

"Because I saw him myself, with my own two eyes, just this morning, and he was right as rain."

CHAPTER 14

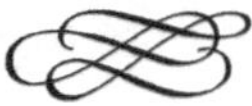

I didn't know how to answer that. Then things got more complicated as Otto started examining the photograph. Not the image on it, but the photograph itself.

"This feels strange," he said, turning it over in his hands. He scratched at the surface with one fingernail. "I've never seen anything like it."

"Crap," I said, mostly to myself. "It's in color."

"I've seen color photos before," he said, giving me an odd look. "Autochrome. It doesn't look like this. And this paper is so light."

I really hadn't thought this plan through. But that wasn't unusual. I was kind of surprised that Brianna hadn't mentioned this flaw when I told her what I was going to do.

"You know we do odd things at the school, right?" I said, holding out my hand for the photograph, but he didn't hand it over.

"There's odd, and then there's this," he said.

"I don't know how much you heard or saw at Cora Fox's house, but surely that was stranger than this," I said.

"That's just what's so odd about it," Otto said. "I would expect you to commune with spirits and channel elemental forces. But this is like a whole different level of technology. Explain."

I bit my lip. I didn't have to tell him anything. If I refused, I was sure he would just accept it. He might be annoyed, but he wasn't going to demand answers.

But I needed his help.

And as much as I wouldn't trust him in a room alone with my valuables, I would trust him to the ends of the Earth with a secret.

"Channel elemental forces," I said. "It's a bit more complicated than that, but that's the gist of it. And the biggest, most important of those forces is time itself."

"Time," Otto said. "Like H.G. Wells."

"Sort of," I said. "Only there's no machine, and we can't just go wherever we want to go. Well, maybe some witches can, I don't know. But Miss Zenobia, she has stabilized a sort of natural formation that creates a bridge across time. One end lies in 1927, the other lies in my own time. I don't have that kind of power myself; I can only travel across it."

"You're not going to tell me when you're from?" he asked.

"2018," I said.

Otto gave a low whistle. "Now I have a million more questions."

"Most of which I can't answer," I said. "Sorry. Apparently, there are rules."

"Which I'd guess you're breaking just by telling me this much," Otto said with a sly grin. "Okay, just one question. Sophie and Brianna. They're also from 2018?"

"Yes," I said.

"That explains it," he said.

"Explains what?"

"The three of you. I know you said you were from out of town, but that didn't really account for all the ways you're just a bit off. Not in a bad way," he was quick to add. "It's just, your accents are strange. Some of the words you use are odd. You even walk a little different from ladies from here and now."

"I didn't know we stuck out so much," I said. "Well, maybe I knew Sophie wasn't blending."

"I doubt she blends into the background anywhere," Otto said.

"That's true," I said.

"I still don't understand how I could have seen Danny Bannon alive this morning when you say he's been dead since last night," Otto said. "Am I not understanding how this bridge works?"

"No, I think you've got it," I said. "It's locked on both ends. The wrinkle is that wardrobe there. It has a separate magic to it. I'm not even sure it exists here. I think it might be in Manhattan right now. All I know is that this man, this Danny Bannon, his dead body turned up in it last night in 2018."

Otto rubbed at his head. "This is hard to follow."

"I could explain it better if I understood it better myself," I sighed.

"So, what did you need from me?" Otto asked.

"His name, which you gave me."

"And nothing else?"

"Well, if you had seen the wardrobe, that might have been a clue," I said. "Bannon was killed by multiple stab wounds, mostly to the chest but a few to the back, particularly over the kidneys. There were two other murders, but I'm not sure they're related. Someone had their head bashed open, and someone else had their throat slit. But given that I don't understand how the time flow works with this wardrobe, those could have happened at any point."

"And you don't have photographs of those people?" Otto asked.

"I never saw the bodies," I said. "I just felt the murders happening."

"You felt..." he trailed off, looking at me closely.

"Witch thing," I said. I didn't explain further, but I didn't need to. I could tell he understood from the sympathy in his eyes.

He looked back down at the photo of Bannon. "Bannon used to be a big deal in town," he told me. "Back before prohibition, when crime was a small-time game. He tried to keep up with the changing times, but it's been obvious for a while now that he doesn't have the stomach for what the new guys do. I've been expecting him to get into a more legit business, but he's trying to hold his turf. A lot of guys would love to kill him and take over his businesses."

"If one of the other gangsters offed him, there could have been two others killed with him. Associates or whatever."

Otto was grinning at my use of the word "gangster," but he summoned a look of seriousness as he nodded his agreement. "Very likely so. He's been edgy. He keeps guys with him to watch his back. He's been getting more paranoid about meeting strangers as well. But if you wanted, I could come up with a pretext to get you into his house."

"I don't think meeting him will do any good," I said.

"I meant to search for that wardrobe," Otto said.

"Oh. Right. That would be helpful."

"You don't sound enthused."

"No, it's a good idea, to look for the wardrobe," I said. "But I don't think I should meet him. Or be in his house when I'm likely to run into him."

"Why? He couldn't possibly recognize you."

"It's not that," I said. "Like I said, there are rules. I can't change what already happened. I know he's going to die. If I meet him, I might inadvertently do something that changes things. Say the wrong thing or just look the wrong way, and he gets a hint that I know his fate."

"I didn't think you were here to save him," Otto said. "I mean, he's always been an all right guy by my book, but somehow I doubt you came from the future to save the life of a lowlife gangster."

"No," I admitted.

"So what is the goal here?" he asked.

"Sophie, Brianna and I have a calling," I said. "The bridge across time can't be taken down, so we three guard it. We protect it from misuse. No one can be allowed to change the flow of time."

"So, you're here for the wardrobe?" he asked.

"No," I sighed. "Honestly? I don't know why I'm here."

"You said the wardrobe worked by its own time rules," Otto said. "If it's not part of the bridge you guard, then it's not part of your job."

"That's right," I said.

"And yet you're here."

I sighed again. This was worse than getting grilled by Nick. "I just want to understand," I said at last.

"So you want the wardrobe to study," he said. "If Bannon turned up in it dead, it might be something he owns now. I've been to his house; it's just the sort of thing he'd own. His wife is very into anything French. The house is a bit of a gilded nightmare, to be honest."

"I can't take it out of the time flow," I said. "It needs to be around in 2018."

"Well, you can take a look at it without destroying all of history, surely," Otto said.

"I suppose," I said glumly.

Otto took a deep breath, then pushed back from his desk to get to his feet. He went to the door, poked his head out and had a few words with Benny, who was still lingering outside. Then he came back to lean against the desk, looking down at me with his arms crossed.

"You should just admit that this is personal to you," he said. "It's not part of your calling."

"I said that," I said defensively.

"But you're not saying what you really want out of this," Otto said. "I can't help you if I don't know what the endgame is."

What was I hoping to accomplish? I couldn't save the dead man, and if he was a criminal, I probably didn't even want to.

"I want answers," I said. The words kept coming out of me, faster than the thoughts could quite form. I had been suppressing these feelings for a while now. "I want to know why it happened, and who the other two victims were. I want to know who did it, and if they are going to do it again. And I suppose this is going to be one of those weird word choices for you, but I want closure."

"Closure," he repeated. "Do you mean revenge?"

"No," I said. "I just want to know it's not going to keep happening."

"You don't want to feel another death," he guessed.

"I don't want to feel another death," I said, little more than a whisper.

"But you can't take the wardrobe away," Otto said.

"I don't think so."

"So the only other way to stop deaths from happening is to get to the source," Otto said. "I can help you with that. And I can make sure the deaths stop."

"But not revenge," I said. "You can't kill anyone on my account. I'm not even really supposed to be here. I'm not of this time."

"But I am," Otto said. "And I don't need a reason to take out someone who's hurting people."

"I don't think it works that way," I said.

There was a soft knock at the door, and Otto pushed away from the desk, extending a hand to help me up from the chair. "Come on," he said.

"Where are we going?" I asked.

"I'm taking you to Bannon's place," he said. "We'll have a look around; see what's going on."

"But no killing," I said.

"I will take no action without your approval," he said.

I let him walk me back out to the street to where his car was ready and waiting, engine already running. He sent a reluctant Benny away, then climbed into the driver's seat himself. I mustered a grateful smile when he looked my way before releasing the parking brake.

But inside, I was more confused than ever. What was I going to be able to do? I couldn't do anything that would change time, and I had no idea what actions that left.

I really regretted going this alone. I needed my fellow witches with me now more than ever.

And yet, I knew if I asked Otto to take me back to the school to fetch the others, he would do it without question. But I wasn't saying those words.

I had a very strong feeling that I had to see this through. I had always been someone who trusted their own gut. As much as I was starting to question that instinct, given how much I was learning about how magic could influence me without me even knowing, I wasn't questioning it enough to rise to the level of real doubt.

But maybe I was getting close.

CHAPTER 15

Otto drove down Summit Avenue, past the charm school, towards the governor's mansion, but turned off and stopped in front of a house about a block off the boulevard.

"This is it," he said, pointing with his chin as he shut off the car's engine. I looked up at the house, a large Tudor style that looked like something out of a book of fairy tales with the icicles hanging from the eaves and the trees and shrubs covered in snow. The upstairs windows were all dark, but two of the downstairs windows were aglow. The curtains were closed so I couldn't see any details within, but occasionally a shadow would pass behind one or the other.

Otto started to open his car door, but I reached out and caught his arm. "Wait," I said.

"I'm just going to take a look," he said, "see who's in there. I won't knock on the door." Then he grinned at me. "I promised no action without your approval."

"Just sit still for a minute," I said. He looked like he wanted to roll his eyes, but he pulled the door shut and sat patiently in the driver's seat, hands resting on the steering wheel.

I sank back into my own seat; the leather still chill despite my body heat. I closed my eyes, took a few measured breaths, then opened my awareness to the world of webs.

Keeping careful hold on the threads that controlled my breathing, I expanded my consciousness out of the car and across the street to focus on the house itself.

As I had suspected, there was no one upstairs, not so much as a child sleeping.

Downstairs was different. I saw five bright clusters of threads moving about. I examined each in turn. None had the feeling of the man who had died inside the wardrobe, Danny Bannon.

Back in the car, I opened my eyes to find Otto watching me intently.

"What?" I asked, touching the back of my gloved hand to my lips in case I had been drooling.

"You were gone," he said.

"And I'm back," I said. "Bannon isn't in there."

"How can you be sure?" he asked.

"I went through the whole house. There are five men in there, but none of them are Bannon. At least, I think they're all men. Their energy felt very masculine to me," I said.

"You went through the whole house," he said.

"That's what I said."

"I believe you," he said. "So Bannon isn't there, but five other guys are. What did they look like?"

"I don't know," I admitted.

"Right," he said, nodding to himself. "You said they felt masculine. Which would be a weird thing to say if you had been looking at them. Witch thing?"

"Witch thing," I agreed.

If someone had told me just a few months ago, I would describe something I did as a "witch thing" with a completely matter-of-fact air, I'm not sure what I would have made of that. Things changed so fast.

"Also, the wardrobe is definitely there. I didn't think it would be, but it is. I sensed it on the second floor."

"They can't be Bannon's bodyguards, since you said Bannon wasn't there," Otto reasoned. "They might work for Bannon and are waiting for a meeting."

"There was a tense feeling of expectancy," I said, remembering the glow to the threads. "They are waiting for something."

"For someone to come, or for it to be time to go," Otto said, tapping his chin as he mulled it over.

"Where could Bannon be?" I asked.

"It's Saturday night," Otto said. "He'll be at the Wabasha Street Speakeasy."

"He'll be out all night," I guessed. Otto gave something between a shrug and a nod. "So we'll wait here for these guys to leave."

"And if they don't leave?" Otto asked.

"Let's assume they will and wait a bit before we ask that question," I said. Otto shrugged again, then turned around to lean into the back seat. He came back with a bearskin blanket and tucked it around both our laps. I slipped my hands beneath it, once more regretting my lack of modern winter gear.

"So, 2018," Otto said conversationally.

"I really can't tell you anything about it," I said. "Sorry."

"Fair enough. I'm just thinking, that explains a bit about you and Edward," he said.

"Me and Edward? There is no me and Edward."

"My point exactly," he said.

"I don't follow," I said.

"Don't be coy. I've seen the way you look at each other. There should be a you and Edward," Otto said with a teasing grin.

"That's not… I've never… well, but Ivy…" My cheeks were getting hot in a way that had nothing to do with the cold air. "The way we look at each other?" I finished lamely.

"You heard me," Otto said.

"You're making trouble," I said.

"I do that," he admitted. "I especially enjoy making trouble for Edward. He's far too comfortable in what shouldn't be his life. But I'm not making trouble now. You know I'm being honest."

"There is Ivy," I persisted.

"Ivy is a misplaced dream," Otto said. "Have you ever even met her?"

"No," I admitted. "Only her sister."

"I've never met her either, but I think we both know her type," he said. "Rich family, correct upbringing, proper social standing. She isn't so much a person as a concept."

"I think that's a terribly unkind thing to say," I said.

"But you know what I mean," he said. "They met at a party, the sort thrown by the best people to mix their offspring together. That's not the place you go to meet a person. That's a place you go to meet a concept."

"You're saying Edward was at that party to find a marriage prospect and he found one," I said. "I don't think it has to be as nefarious as you put it."

"It's maybe a class thing. My people don't throw such parties," he said, then looked irked as I laughed.

"Sorry, but you do realize that you just said that in your lower-class voice," I said.

"I only have the one," he said darkly.

"Oh, no, you don't, Mr. I've read H.G. Wells," I said. "To be fair, I'm guessing you talk that way most of the time to most people you meet. You talked that way when I first met you. But when you're around the three of us, and I suspect even when you're just around Edward, you let your education show a bit."

"That's a filthy lie," he said, but I knew he was joking with me.

"Edward isn't the only one looking to move up in the world," I said.

"Yeah, but I'm looking to do it honestly," Otto said.

"Through crime?"

"Through crime. But not through marriage," he said.

"I'm guessing Edward feels differently about that distinction," I said.

"That's because he's deluding himself," Otto said. I could hear the frustration and almost anger in his voice. "That family will never have him. They're playing him for a fool."

"They're using him?" I asked, confused.

"He's young, charming, and eager to please. When you have a squadron of young men courting your oldest daughter, it's nice to have such a fellow around to force the lazier ones to try a bit harder."

"Wow," I said. "You really do see nefarious plots everywhere."

"I'm not wrong," Otto said. "Ivy McTavet will never be Mrs. Edward Scott."

"Have you told Edward how you feel?" I asked. Otto scoffed. "I don't mean how you're clearly missing him now that he works in a bank all day and not running schemes with you anymore. Or how you know you'll see him even less if he marries into a respectable family. I mean, about your suspicions."

"No," he said, studying a small imperfection on his car's dashboard.

"You should," I said. "Especially if you're right. He should be warned."

"You think I'm right?" he asked, still not looking at me.

"About your feelings?" I asked, only half teasing, but if I said it seriously again, he'd probably get out of the car and just walk away from me. "I don't know."

"You could find out if I was right," he said.

"I could," I admitted. "Maybe it would be better if I did. I could read up on all the local history and find out the fate of everyone I've encountered in 1927. I would know who they married, when they died, maybe even if they were happy. But having those facts would mean not really being able to get to know them as people. I don't want every conversation I have with Coco to be under the specter of knowing her entire fate."

"It must be tempting, though," Otto said.

"More than you know," I sighed. How many times had I been distracted from my own studying by the temptation to look through the old newspapers for Edward's name?

"It's not just her family, though," Otto said after a long moment's silence. "It's Edward. He's worked hard to get to where he is. He's left his past behind. I'm not bitter about that; I think it's wonderful. He looks like a young businessman on his way up in the world because that's who he is. But he's gotten it in his head that the next step up is marrying and having a father-in-law to fill in for the father he never knew. And he doesn't need it."

"Tell him that," I said, but he just shook his head.

"I'm just trying to explain that Ivy to him is a concept. If he had met her somewhere else, didn't know who she was or who her family was, just found himself smitten by her wonderful self, I wouldn't say a thing. But he's not attached to the person. He's attached to the concept. That will never be a happy marriage."

"Well," I said, scrambling for words. Something about how love can grow over time, maybe. But he didn't wait for me to gather his thoughts.

"I've never met Ivy, that's true. I've never seen Edward and her together. But I know Edward. He doesn't love Ivy."

"I don't know," I said. "I've seen him talk about her. He lights up."

"With ambition, maybe," Otto said. "Look, Edward is a decent guy. He can't be otherwise. He's not going to have a wife and something else on the side. So I know he can't possibly ever have looked at Ivy with real love in his eyes. Because I've seen him look at you."

I had no answer for that. Even if I had, my heart was pounding so hard I don't think I could get the words out. It was all I could do to keep my breathing under control.

Hey, I'd found another use for Sophie's meditation practices. Thwarting emotional reactions to just the things you'd been secretly dying to hear.

"That doesn't matter," I said when I, at last, had myself mostly under control. "He should be with Ivy, and I wish them every happiness. Because he can't be with me."

"Because of the time thing," Otto said.

"Yes," I said, and my cheeks were burning again. "But not just that. There's another, um, fellow."

"Oh, yes?" Otto said with dripping skepticism.

"Yes," I said, raising my chin. "Obviously, I can't tell Edward about that. Not without explaining the time thing, which he really shouldn't know. But there is someone I've been seeing. Someone I'm fond of."

Otto scoffed again, louder than before.

"You don't know me," I said angrily.

"Please," Otto said. "You are just like Edward. Too honorable to be messing with two fellows at once. Whoever this guy is, I'm sure he's all kinds of wonderful, but I'll never believe you look at him the way you look at Edward."

"You sure put a lot of stock in looks," I said, getting annoyed. "Feelings are feelings. We can't control those. All we control is our actions. I can't be with Edward. I'm not taking any action that says otherwise."

"Fair enough," Otto said. "I'll be watching you. I'll keep you honest."

"Thanks much, but I can police my own behavior."

Otto shrugged, then shifted in his seat. "It looks like our lurkers are finally heading out."

I sat up in my own seat, watching as five men in wool coats and fancy hats walked down the recently shoveled walk and dispersed themselves among the two cars parked at the curb about half a block away.

"Right," Otto said, opening his car door. "Let's go."

CHAPTER 16

*A*fter several long, fruitless minutes, Otto swore under his breath, then straightened up, stuffing his lock picks back into his pocket.

"I'll just break a window," he said and started kicking through the snow around the shrubs in search of a rock.

"Hold on," I said, checking all my pockets. I found the gold key in my dress pocket. "I have something quieter."

"That's not the right size for this door," Otto said, but now it was my turn to grin at him.

"Trust me," I said. I pushed the key into the lock and gave it a turn.

"Can I have that?" he asked as I swung the door open.

"No way," I said, tucking the key away.

"Can you make me a copy?"

"No," I said, laughing. "Come on; let's get inside before someone sees us."

"No one is around to see us," he said, but followed me into the darkness of the front hall. When he closed the door behind us, that darkness became total. "Do you have a spell for this?" he asked.

"Maybe," I said, reaching for my wand. I knew I could do it, but I also knew it would be draining.

"Forget about it," Otto said. "I've got this one." There was a click, and then a beam of light shot past me to illuminate the stairway in front of us.

He'd brought a flashlight and lock picks. And I hadn't seen him grab any of those things on the way out of his speakeasy. Those were apparently just the sorts of things he always had in his pockets.

"You said the wardrobe was upstairs?" he said as he shone his light up the steps.

"Up, to the left, back of the house," I said. "Bedroom maybe?"

Otto nodded, then started up the stairs. I followed behind, stepping as softly as I could even though I knew the house was empty. Otto's feet made no sound on the bare wooden stairs either, but then a man who always carried lock picks with him probably also always walked silently through strange houses at night.

We turned to the left at the top of the stairs and followed the hallway until it ended at a pair of doors. Otto gently turned the handle on the door to the right, the one that led to the room at the back side of the house. He shone his light all around the space, then crossed the room to secure the shade over the room's only window. Then he gave me a nod, and I flipped on the light switch.

It was a bedroom, but it didn't look like it saw much use. There was nothing personal sitting on the dresser or nightstand, and the bed was neatly made but didn't look freshly so.

The wardrobe stood against the wall to my right. There was a wide space between it and the side of the bed, as if whoever had arranged the furniture had, for some reason, left a huge gap in the room there.

"Look at the floor," Otto said, pointing at the bare floorboards. "There's a rug missing."

I bent to get a closer look. The floor was free of dust, but there was a faint outline of an oval shape as if something had protected that part of the wooden floor from the bleaching effects of the sun.

"Why would someone take the rug out of here?" I wondered. "It doesn't look like anyone even uses this room."

"Well, since we're dealing with three suspected murders, I know what leaps to my mind," Otto said.

I looked up at the wardrobe.

"What does it mean that you're here and not in Manhattan?" I asked it.

It towered over me, but said nothing.

Otto opened a door in the corner of the room and peered into an empty closet, then shut the door again.

"I'm going to try a few things here," I said. "It's going to look to you like what I did in the car."

"Ugh," he said. I shot him a quizzical look. "Dead bodies don't creep me out the way that did. You were looking at me, but you weren't there."

"I thought my eyes were closed," I said.

"They were until I said your name," Otto said with a shudder. "I never should have called your name. But you were breathing really weird. Like, mechanical."

"I had no idea," I said, and in my mental to-do list, I double-underlined going into the web world with Brianna and/or Sophie watching over me. Apparently, I hadn't quite finessed it yet. "Maybe you should go out? I mean of the room, not the house. Be my lookout while I'm occupied."

"And how am I supposed to warn you if I need to?" he asked.

"I'm not sure," I admitted. "Just improvise. Hopefully, if there is genuine danger, I'll be aware."

"I'm only saying yes because I want to snoop around," he said. "Don't take long."

"I'll try not to," I said, then added as he was going out the door, "and don't steal anything!"

"Just snooping," he shouted back. But I couldn't read his face to know if he was telling the truth or not.

I opened the wardrobe doors wide, then made a search of the stack of smaller drawers up one side of the inside space, then two wider drawers on the bottom.

Nothing. Save for some balls of dust; it was completely empty.

It looked vulnerable with its doors open. I gently shut them again before sitting down on the floor in front of it. I was acutely aware of the absence of rug. Perhaps it was needed in some other part of the house, but I doubted it. Otto's idea that it was related to the murders felt more right to me. Even if there had been no need to roll up a body inside of it, it would have gotten stained when the body was stuffed into the wardrobe.

Assuming the murder wasn't actually committed right where I was sitting.

I suppressed a shudder, then closed my eyes and dropped into my meditative state.

The wardrobe stood before me, its threads glowing brightly with the inner fire of an enchanted object. It was a brighter glow here than in 2018.

There was also a strange truncation to some of its threads as if they had been severed and then retracted protectively deep within its matrix. Was this because its sister wardrobe had recently been burned to ash in Paris? It felt that way. When my consciousness brushed over the cut ends, I felt a profound sadness.

But the wardrobe wasn't sentient. Unlike the crystal ball, it couldn't communicate with me.

I searched it for any stray threads that related to Danny Bannon. I found a few. Nothing large enough to tell me any details, but enough to know he had been inside this wardrobe recently.

There were other traces as well. Two other people, I thought, but I couldn't get a real picture of who they were. Maybe they were just previous owners of the wardrobe, leaving an imprint behind like Nick had in his room back in his grandfather's apartment.

I made another thorough search but turned up no more clues, so I returned to my body and opened my eyes.

Had I just been breathing mechanically? I felt a little lightheaded, now that I was really thinking about it, although I would have thought that would just come from doing that magic.

I looked at the wardrobe again in the warm light from the fixture over the door.

"I wish you could tell me your story," I said, pressing my palms to the wood. I opened the doors again to make one more search for any sign that this piece of furniture had been bled all over and then methodically cleaned.

There was no sign of blood anywhere, but I did find a slip of paper in one of the drawers that hadn't been there before. I stepped back to look at it in better light before unfolding it.

There were only three words on it in a spidery script that looked so perfect in line and spacing I would have thought it was printed from a computer. It said, "Je suis désolé." That was all.

One of the French sisters trying to apologize to the other? But which one? And how had the note gone astray? Perhaps the reason their parlor trick act had failed was that the witch they consulted for time magic didn't have the control she thought she did. What disappeared in one wardrobe would appear in either wardrobe at any time, completely at random.

That would be a terrible show. Especially if Sephora was right, and they had started using people.

What a horrid thought.

I put the note in my pocket and shut the wardrobe doors. Then I turned out the bedroom light and slipped back down the hall, looking for signs of Otto's flashlight.

I found him in a room off the front hall. From the looks of it, this was Danny Bannon's office. Otto was sitting behind the desk, running his hands over the wood.

"I didn't learn anything useful," I said as I watched him. It looked like he was searching for hidden compartments. "Do you know if he's dead yet?"

"I'm not sure," he said, then pointed with his chin at a photograph on the corner of his desk. "If he is, I think I might know who the other two victims are."

I picked up the photograph. Danny Bannon, I recognized at once. With him was a rosy-cheeked woman with her hair combed back in sleek waves and a boy with an overabundance of freckles that, even in black and white, looked like they had been exacerbated by an impressive sunburn.

"His family?" I said, setting the photograph back down. "I liked the henchmen theory better."

Otto shrugged. It was all the same to him, apparently.

Then something clicked, and he said something in German I was sure meant "Eureka."

"What is it?" I asked.

"Ledgers," he said, reaching into the open space by his knee and pulling out a series of leather-bound notebooks.

"That will tell you if he's living or dead?" I asked.

"It's the best clue to who might have killed him," he said, flipping through the pages.

"I would assume there'd be some sort of code," I said.

"There is, but it's to confound the government building a case against him, not for the likes of me," Otto said. "Plus, the man who taught me everything I know about the business first learned it from Danny Bannon. And like I said, he's not changing with the times."

"So you can read that?" I asked. I could tell what the numbers meant, but the words that were attached to them were unpronounce-able jumbled anagrams.

Otto didn't answer me, focusing on the finger he was tracing down the last column of numbers on the last page of the book. He looked up at me, and his face had gone grayish-white.

"What is it?" I asked.

"We have to get out of here, now," he said, shutting the books, then tucking them inside his coat.

"Bannon is still alive?" I asked as we fast-walked across the front hall to the door.

"No, definitely not," Otto said grimly. "I know who killed him. I'll explain later. First, we get to safety."

I wasn't about to argue with that. As he reached out to pull open the heavy front door, my fingers were already reaching for my wand. Because it felt better to have it in my hand.

But before he had quite touched that doorknob or I my wand, the door blew open, hitting the wall with a crash and throwing us both back onto the tiled floor. The men from before were back, and they had a woman with them.

And I didn't need to go to the web world to sense her magical power. She was radiating it out of her body as if she had no worries about running out or growing tired from the effort.

She was a witch, but nothing like any witch I had yet met.

And my fallen wand was on the floor at her feet.

CHAPTER 17

I blinked away my awareness of her magic as the woman strode towards me. I think it was a spell; she was deliberately trying to dazzle me so I couldn't see her.

A handy spell if you ran with gangsters. Anyone asking for a description of the suspect gets nothing useful back. A woman, average height and weight, hair that was maybe blonde or brown, no distinguishing features. Nothing that would ever lead anyone back to her.

But I squinted until I did see her. Blond hair in a bob with the curls arranged to frame her face just so, eyes of an icy shade of blue that was quite distinctive, a little mole just below the corner of one eye.

"Little witch," she said as she stopped walking to stand over me.

I realized I was shading my eyes as I looked up at her and forced my hand back down.

"What's a witch doing here?" one of the men asked.

"I really have no idea," she said in a singsong voice.

"Tommy won't like it," he said.

"Tommy doesn't like lots of things," she said with a shrug. "Perhaps it's not even his affair. Perhaps I should just take her to my employer."

"Not without Tommy's go ahead first," he said with a warning tone.

Two of the other men were standing near the door as if guarding it, although whether to keep us in or someone else out, I couldn't tell. The other two were both standing over Otto with guns drawn. Otto had his hands raised to show he was unarmed.

"Vinnie, that's Otto Mayer," one of the other men said.

"Otto Mayer?" the man next to the witch said, then shifted his attention from me to Otto. "Never heard of him."

"You know him," the other guy insisted. "He runs that gang of thieving brats."

Vinnie swept his gaze up and down Otto's sprawled form. "I don't think so. That gang is run by a teenager, and this is no teenager."

"Your buddy has old information," Otto said. "I did run that gang when I was younger."

"Oh, yes?" Vinnie asked with exaggerated boredom. "And now?"

"Now I run the Greasy Spoon," Otto said.

"That's the speakeasy behind the—" the other man started to say.

"I know what the Greasy Spoon is," Vinnie snapped. Then he turned back to Otto. "It's a terrible name."

"I just took possession a few days ago," Otto said with a forced laugh. "Give a guy a chance to get his feet under him before he goes changing the nomenclature."

Just then my stomach clenched into a hard, hot knot so tight and painful I couldn't draw a breath. I gasped as black stars exploded before my eyes.

"What's with her?" Vinnie asked.

"I can't even imagine," the woman said, looking down at me with a smile. She waited for my vision to clear, for me to see my wand in her hands before she tucked it away in her coat pocket.

My wand. She had my wand.

She had touched my wand. Wow, Brianna had said letting another witch touch my wand would be upsetting, but she hadn't told me the half of it.

"I really should take her to my employer," the witch said, turning to direct all her attention on Vinnie. He flinched but didn't look away.

"Not until Tommy says okay," he said. I could see him steel his resolve, but it wavered again the moment she rested her hand on his arm.

Her lips parted. But whatever she had been about to say, or whatever spell she had been about to cast to make poor Vinnie do her bidding, I would never know. Because just at that moment, the door swung open again and a final man stepped into the front hall.

One of the other men rushed forward to take his cane and hat, another to help him shrug off his coat. He was dressed much like Otto, in all the finery but with an air of not being used to it. The clothes were all new, and they must have been tailored just to his frame because they fit him exactly. Which couldn't have been easy to pull off; he was built like a wrestler: short but muscled all over in great bulging masses, with a chest like a barrel.

"Hello, Tommy," the witch cooed as she moved easily from Vinnie to this new arrival.

"Evanora," he said coldly. He didn't like her, was, in fact, a little afraid of her, but was trying not to show it. Probably the smart move.

"What needs my okay?" he asked, barely sparing a glance at Otto and me still sprawled on the floor.

"My employer will be very interested in this little witch," Evanora said, waving a hand my way. Tommy fixed his gaze on me. His brown eyes were so dark I couldn't tell pupil from iris.

"That's a witch," he said as if he didn't quite believe it. "What's she doing here?"

"I'm sure we'll find out soon enough," Evanora said. "You know my employer doesn't hold anything back with you."

"Erm, yes," Tommy said, still gazing steadily at me. But then he looked up at Evanora, and his eyes hardened. "No, I'll question her. She's in my house. That's my business."

"But Tommy—" she started to object.

"No, I insist," he said, and she closed her mouth and gave him an indulgent smile. "Just until I get to the bottom of all this. When I'm done with her, she's all yours."

"When you're done with her, is there going to be anything left?" Evanora asked, her voice almost a purr.

Tommy laughed. "A few scraps, I'm sure," he said. Evanora just kept smiling at him with that enigmatic smile until his laughter died away. "Tell your employer I'll turn her over to you just as soon as I know what's going on here. Unharmed. Tell her that. My promise." He touched a hand to his chest where his heart ought to be.

Evanora gave a little nod and turned towards the door.

"Hold on," Vinnie said, stepping in front of her and holding out his hand.

"Why do you detain me?" she asked with false sweetness.

"You took something from her. Give it back," he said, thrusting his hand at her.

Evanora sighed and looked to Tommy.

"Hand it over," Tommy said without looking at her. He was looking at Otto, or more specifically Otto's chest. He leaned over and thrust Otto's coat aside to retrieve the ledgers. He gave Otto a triumphant grin and started paging through the first ledger when he noticed that Vinnie and Evanora were still having their standoff. "I gave my word. This girl and everything she has with her will be your employer's soon enough."

Evanora mulled that over for a moment, then pulled my wand out of her pocket.

Another stab of liquid heat and searing pain through my guts as she placed it in Vinnie's hand. Vinnie stuffed it in his own pocket and only then could I draw breath again.

"What's with her?" Tommy asked, looking at me with a frown.

"Unharmed, Mr. Nielsen," Evanora said.

"Yes, yes, enough already," Tommy said, waving her away dismissively. "I gave my word once. Saying it over and over doesn't make it any more binding."

"Are you sure about that?" Evanora asked. Then that Cheshire cat grin spread over her face again and she slipped out of the door, disappearing into the winter night.

"Amanda?" Otto called to me. I had curled up on my side, arms wrapped around my still-aching middle.

"I'm okay," I said.

I wasn't, though. Neither of us were.

"Bring them into my study," Tommy said, eyes once more on the pages of the ledger. He crossed the hall towards Danny Bannon's office. Vinnie made a waving motion, and the other four guys split up, two each grabbing Otto and me by the arms and dragging us to our feet.

The two guys holding my arms pushed me into a chair near the door and used my own scarf to tie me to it so tightly my hands and feet started to go numb at once. Then they tipped the chair back on its back legs and pivoted it around so that I was staring at the wall, the rest of the office behind me.

I had a brief glimpse of Otto being tied to the chair across the desk from where Tommy stood, and of Vinnie stoking up the fire in the fireplace along the far wall, and then I was looking at nothing but dark wood paneling and a painting of a fox hunt back in Merry Olde England.

I heard the sound of the ledgers snapping shut and then Tommy said, "Otto Mayer."

"Tommy Nielsen," Otto sneered back. "You've killed Danny Bannon."

"Did I?" Tommy said blandly.

"We're standing in his house, which you keep referring to as yours," Otto said.

"Only one of us is standing, boyo," Tommy said.

One of the men who had tied me up walked out of the door. I could just see it out of the corner of my eye. The other leaned against the wall with his arms folded, his shoulder just brushing against the hunting painting. He wasn't watching me, or at least not closely. His eyes were on his boss.

"You know what I mean," Otto said, his voice a low rumble. There was a rattling sound, and I imagined him rocking his chair as he tested his bonds.

"No, leave him," Tommy said, I imagined to one of the other henchmen. "You're not wrong about this being my house," he went on. "As I'm sure you worked out from the ledgers—honestly, what's the point of using a code if it's one everyone who's ever worked under you knows?—Bannon owed me really a frightful amount of money. So I took his house. Fair's fair."

"He was lying about how much he owed you," Otto said.

"Yes, he was," Tommy said, and some of the jocularity had faded from his tone. "So yes, I took his life."

I heard a low moan and realized it was coming from me.

But there was no way this gangster was going to confess to murder and just let us go.

Or I suppose he was going to let me go, turn me over to Evanora's mysterious employer. I didn't know what that would entail. I sensed nothing good.

But I knew that Otto would be dead.

"That was a bad call," Otto said. "Bannon was worthless, had been for years, but he played by the rules. But you? You broke the rules. And you'll have to pay."

"I broke no rules," Tommy said.

"You murdered Bannon. You just said so," Otto said.

"I said no such thing," Tommy scoffed.

"You murdered him here, in his house. Then you stole this house. This house which lies nicely within the boundaries of the city of St. Paul," Otto said. I had no idea why that was important, but from the way the man leaning against the wall in front of me just stiffened up, it was important.

"I did no such thing," Tommy said, whispering now.

"You broke the rules," Otto said with a humorless laugh. "You broke O'Connor's rules, and when Dapper Dan finds out, you'll be a dead man."

"That's what the two of you were doing here? Digging dirt for Dapper Dan?" Tommy asked.

"You killed Bannon. Dapper Dan had a soft spot for Bannon," Otto said.

"You have no proof," Tommy said.

"You killed Bannon and his wife and his wee lad. How old was he? Nine? If that?" Otto asked. No one answered him, but the silence in the rest of the room was oppressive. "You killed them one after the other. Bam, head smashed. Swish, throat slit. Tick, tick, tick, all of you getting a stab in on our friend Bannon."

"You have no proof," Tommy said, a dangerous edge to his voice.

But Otto wouldn't take the hint to stop talking. "You ditched the rug, good call. No evidence there. But you stuffed them all in that wardrobe, and that was really your mistake, wasn't it? How long was it before you discovered those bodies were gone?"

There was a crash of noise, and I had no idea what was going on. I tried to get to my feet, to turn my chair around, but the man near me leaned a hand on the back of my chair, pinning it back down.

Then Otto started to scream.

CHAPTER 18

The sound of that scream, filled with fear and pain that I could never imagine coming out of Otto; it was like it just pushed me out of my body.

I don't think I even closed my eyes. I didn't grab the threads to connect to my body either. It was like the form of me that inhabited the web world was running in crazed panic.

I stopped in front of the wardrobe, and only then managed to get a hold of myself.

The wardrobe couldn't help me. It didn't have a mind of its own. I was without allies.

But I didn't need it as an ally. Not when I could use it as a tool.

I slipped inside the glow of its living threads and gathered them around me. Then I started swinging my doors open and slamming them shut, over and over. I clattered my drawers. I even made my feet dance heavily on the floor.

The bedroom wasn't over the office where everyone else was, but it was close enough. They could hear me. Someone would come to investigate.

And someone did. One of the nameless henchmen was in the

doorway, looking in at me, his fear palpable. But he didn't give in to it. He crept forward, gun at the ready for all the good it would do.

I stopped moving. I was an inert, completely normal wardrobe, just standing there with my doors open invitingly.

The man came closer, keeping the gun raised as his other hand reached out to close my doors.

He didn't trip. I don't know quite what happened, but in the next instant he was tumbling into me, falling into the space inside that was barely large enough to contain him.

And in the instant after that, he was quite gone.

I searched every thread, but I saw no sign of where he had disappeared to. He had left a few bits of himself behind, clues that he had been there, that he had existed, which only I could see. For the rest of the world, he was erased as if he had never been. Like Danny Bannon and his family.

I started up the noise again. At some point, someone was going to come up the stairs with an axe or something, but until then, every man I lured away was another man not making Otto scream.

But something funny was happening. I kept feeling like I wasn't sure if I was there or not. One moment I was perceiving the web world, manipulating the threads of the enchanted wardrobe around me. Then the next was nothing but blackness.

I tried to focus, to keep myself anchored where I chose to be.

Oh, *anchored*. The thing I hadn't done with my corporeal form.

The darkness closed around me as if I were slowly being plunged into a cold mass of thick goo.

Then I was awake, horridly awake, every detail around me too sharp. I tried to push away the thing under my nose, but my hands were still tied.

I glared up at the man standing over me. He took the vial away and put it back in his pocket. Then he looked past me to I supposed either Tommy or Vinnie.

"She's back," the man said. "Unharmed."

"Was she doing...?" Tommy started to ask, then changed his mind. "Forget it. Vinnie, get back to work."

Otto had been taking loud, jagged breaths that whole time. Now he was screaming once more. His voice was already sounding hoarse. Broken, really. If his voice couldn't hold out much longer, what about his body?

And they weren't even asking him any questions.

Otto inhaled sharply, and I thought I heard the sound of someone moving closer to him. I twisted my hands, trying to squirm my way free, but my captors had too much experience with knots, even using scarves.

"Tommy Nielsen," Otto said through gritted teeth. "Don't you want to know where those bodies went to? They could turn up anywhere, and then where would you be?"

"Boss?" one of the other henchmen asked. "Where did those bodies go?"

"Shut it," Tommy snapped. "He's messing with your head."

"Those bodies just disappearing like that is what's messing with my head," the henchman grumbled. "That wardrobe was never out of my sight, not even for a second. But when we opened it up on the bridge, it was empty. Not even a drop of blood. And there should have been a lot of blood."

"I told you to shut it," Tommy said again, more loudly this time.

The henchman standing over me made eye contact with someone behind me and gave a little shake to his head.

"But what if they trace them back to us, Stu?" the henchman asked. He was standing just out of my sight, whispering to the man in front of me.

"Come on, Mikey. The boss has this under control. Why do you think he brought the witches into it?" Stu whispered back.

"Oh, yeah. Right," Mikey said.

"Why don't you just let me shoot him?" Vinnie asked.

"Because he threatened me," Tommy said in a low growl. "No one threatens me. I'm going to put his head on a pike for all to see what happens to fellas that try to threaten me."

"Boss," Vinnie said in his most soothing voice. "He's threatening to go to Dapper Dan because you broke the O'Connor rules. If you put his head on a pike, you'll be doing that message-sending for him. We can't kill him here."

"Fine," Tommy snapped. "Rob, bring the car around."

"Right, boss," Rob said.

"Wait," Vinnie said, and I heard a scuffle as if he had caught Rob by the arm before he could leave. "Where are you going?"

"I'm not going anywhere," Tommy said. "You five can take him out to some nice, quiet little township out in the middle of nowhere, finish him off, and leave the body. That's the O'Connor rules nicely observed."

"People know I'm here," Otto said. "They'll come looking for me."

"Well, since your most powerful friend was Danny Bannon, you'll pardon me for not quaking in my boots."

"You four," I said. It seemed to take a tremendous amount of energy to get those words out. What I had done with the wardrobe had taxed me greatly. I couldn't let it mean nothing.

"What'd she say?" Tommy asked.

"She said 'you four'," Stu said, looking around the room. "She's right. There's just four of us besides you."

"Johnny is in the hall watching out the front door," Tommy said. "You can take him with you when you go. I don't need a babysitter."

"Are you sure?" I asked.

"Stu, can't you shut her up?" Tommy asked, exasperated.

"Without harming her?" Stu asked.

"Don't be such a namby-pamby. There's harm, and then there's *harm*. An attitude-adjusting smack isn't harm," he said.

"Don't touch her," Otto said. "You'll regret it."

"Says the man tied to the chair," Vinnie sneered.

Otto grunted in pain. Then the grunt became a continuous groan that finally broke free into a scream.

The only thing growing faster was my own anger. I could feel it in my chest like some hot-blooded, pulsating parasite that was squeezing my heart and making my vision turn a lurid shade of red.

I had had enough. I focused on that anger and let it drive the weariness out of my bones. It burned the fog from my brain. My thoughts were suddenly clearer.

But I couldn't take another second of Otto's screams of pain.

"Stop hurting him," I said over my shoulder. I didn't shout, but I spoke clearly enough for everyone still in that room to hear me.

"Shut up," Stu said.

I glared up at him, then gave him my best manic grin. "You don't want to make me angry."

"You don't scare me," he said.

"Where's your friend?" I asked him. "The one in the hall? John, was it? The one who went upstairs to see what all the noise was about?"

He shifted his weight from foot to foot, then looked up at someone standing behind me. Probably not Mikey again; he seemed like he was looking for a management decision from Vinnie or Tommy.

"Ignore her," Tommy said. "Gag her if you have to."

"That won't stop me," I said as Stu started pulling off his own scarf.

"You can't hurt me," he said, but he was hesitating to draw nearer to me.

"Because you have me tied up?" I asked. My hands and feet were like cold, dead weights now. Even if I got myself untied, I'd be pretty helpless.

"Because Vinnie has your wand," he said. "A witch is just like any other dame without her wand."

"You're wrong," I said. "*You're* the one who can't hurt *me*."

"Because of Evanora? The boss can handle Evanora," he said.

"Not Evanora," I said. "Evanora's employer."

He blanched at that, and I really wished I knew what I was talking about. Who was this mysterious employer?

Then he got himself back under control, the scarf drawn tight between his hands as he moved in to tie it around my mouth.

"But you're wrong about the wand thing as well," I said quickly. "I don't need it."

"Sure you don't," he said with a smirk.

Then my mouth was full of the taste of wet wool; the fibers itching my tongue.

And through all of that, Otto was still writhing in pain.

I struggled against my bonds again, but only because the feel of the scarf tightening around my wrists and ankles, the bite of that pain, it fueled the angry beast inside my chest.

And then the anger took over.

This time I deliberately didn't close my eyes. I just pushed myself into my altered state, never breaking eye contact with Stu standing over me.

My vision was suddenly doubled. I saw the world as I normally did, but superimposed on that were the living threads.

My scarf and Stu's scarf were both wool, something that had once been alive. That made their threads easier for me to see and manipulate than if they had been inorganic.

It was ridiculously easy to break the threads. The scarves both crumbled into little fibrous puff balls and blew away.

I stood up. Stu fell back against the wall. The look on his face was abject terror. Somehow, I doubted that was just from me magicking my bonds away. It seemed extreme for even what Otto had described before.

I stepped forward and felt a surge of delight as he cowered back from me. I felt power coursing through me. The threads that made up my body were glowing brighter than a thousand enchanted objects.

"Please," Stu said, trying to cover his head with his arms. "Don't hurt me."

"Why would I hurt you?" I asked.

I was pretty accustomed to finding the threads that corresponded to lungs by now. It was such a simple thing to reach into Stu's chest, catch hold of those threads, and just tweak them a little.

Stu's eyes rolled up into his head, his knees buckled, and I stepped back as he fell to the floor with a crash.

Then I turned around.

I looked at the chaos of threads that made up the room. Otto, in all of his pain and agony, was the centerpiece. His threads were flashing like a warning light, a warning light with a dying bulb. Vinnie stood over him. Hurting him.

Tommy was turned away, pretending not to pay attention.

Neither of them noticed that I was free, nor that Stu was lying on the floor.

Then the other two came back in the room. Mikey and Rob.

"We got the car, but we can't find John," Rob started to say, but Mikey talked right over him.

"What's with Stu?"

It was almost as if they didn't see me. But they were between me and Otto. I stepped up to them and plunged a hand into each of them.

They saw me then, their eyes widening in terror just before they too collapsed to the floor.

"Knock her out!" Tommy demanded. I spun to turn my attention to him, but then a hand closed over my nose and mouth, an arm wrapping around my throat. Vinnie. I didn't struggle; I just smiled at Tommy.

I mean, he couldn't see since my mouth was covered, but I think he knew. He could see it in my eyes.

I had to reach through my own body to get to Vinnie. I had to take my time with it, to be sure not to get tangled up in any of my own threads.

Vinnie gasped at my touch. For a moment, his grip on me tightened. I wasn't breathing at the moment, but I felt a vague worry that he was going to snap my neck.

Then his arm loosened, and he too fell to the floor.

I almost faltered then. The anger was starting to burn itself out. Perhaps if I had been the sort of person to nurse grudges, I would be better at this sort of magic.

What was I thinking? Who wanted to be good at this sort of magic?

Now the power was flowing out of me like water from a punctured kiddie pool. I grasped at it, summoned every bit of my will, and caught a hold of enough to break the once-living threads that made up the rope of Otto's bonds.

I wasn't sure if that would do any good, as hurt as he was.

I felt a sudden pain in my knees and realized I had collapsed. I looked down at my hands, purple-tinged from being tied too tightly for too long, but perfectly ordinary.

The double vision of two realities at once was gone. So was the anger.

I heard Otto yell and looked up to see him in mid-leap over Bannon's desk. That hadn't been a yell of pain that time; it had been a battle cry.

Tommy screamed, but couldn't run away before Otto was on top of him.

"Always start with the fingers," Otto growled at him, taking one of Tommy's fingers and, without warning, snapping it with a sickening crunch. "If you're going to hurt a man, be sure he can't hurt you back."

"No!" Tommy shrieked, and I flinched away from the sound of another finger bone snapping.

"Otto, stop," I said.

"Me stop?" he barked a laugh at me. "You've killed all the others!"

"They're not dead," I said, although I wasn't sure about the one I had fed to the wardrobe. "I just stopped their breathing for a moment. They've passed out, but they'll be fine."

"You scare me," Otto said. I looked into his eyes and saw that this was true. He was a mess of blood from a thousand shallow cuts, but that was part of a world he understood.

I was part of another world altogether.

"We should get out of here," I said, although I felt too weary to even get up off the floor.

"We have to finish this," Otto said.

"I don't want to kill anyone," I said.

"Listen to her," Tommy said. He moved as if he wanted to sit up but Otto, still straddling his center of gravity, pushed him back down to the floor. "Remember the O'Connor rules."

"What are the O'Connor rules?" I asked.

"Something the St. Paul chief of police set up years ago," Otto said. "Criminals in St. Paul won't be hounded for their crimes, provided their crimes don't happen inside St. Paul. You can run liquor over the border from Canada, rob banks in Minneapolis, kill people on some lonely stretch of road between here and Rochester, but as long as you behave in St. Paul city limits, the police here won't bother you."

"That's messed up," I said. "And this Dapper Dan fellow enforces this?"

"He works with the police, yeah," Otto said.

"And if Dapper Dan knew what Tommy here had done?"

"He'd be a dead man," Otto said, leering down at Tommy.

I sighed. So tired. "And if you just reported him to the St. Paul police?"

"They'd talk to Dapper Dan," Otto said. "What outcome are you looking for here?"

"Justice?" I said.

"Justice would be shoving him inside that wardrobe," Otto said.

"Please don't," Tommy said, hands raised.

"These are bad people, Amanda. They're not going to stop being bad people just because you tell them to."

"I can't risk changing time," I said.

"I'll do it," Otto said.

"No," I said.

"Amanda, if I don't take him out now, he'll be back for me," Otto said.

"I won't," Tommy pleaded.

"Shut up, you," Otto growled.

"No, you're right," I said. Even I could see that Tommy wasn't going to let a grudge go.

Vinnie on the floor beside me started to stir.

"We have to get out of here," I said, trying again to push myself to my feet. This time I managed it. "Tommy," I said in my most commanding voice. "You're not going to hurt Otto. You're, in fact, going to be sure that no one ever hurts Otto. Because if Otto is ever hurt, I'm going to come for you. Me and my fellow witches. What I just did here was nothing. They have far more power than I could ever hope for. Don't cross us."

"Amanda, that's not going to be enough," Otto pleaded.

"It will have to be," I said. But then I had another thought. "Tommy, you're going to get out of town. St. Paul isn't for you anymore. Pack up and move."

"Amanda…" Otto said warningly.

"Where?" Tommy asked, eager to please.

"Manhattan," I sighed. "And take that wardrobe with you. Come on, Otto. Time to go."

Otto looked like he wanted to argue, but in the end, he just leaned close into Tommy's face. "I'll be watching for you to go. Then I'm telling everything to Dapper Dan. You'll never be welcome here again."

"I'll go," Tommy promised.

Otto rapped Tommy's head on the floor hard enough to leave him dazed, then stood up and walked over to me.

I bent to reach inside Vinnie's coat and found my wand.

My stomach roiled again, not liking the touch of my own wand. I stuffed it inside my own coat and tried not to despair over how much better I felt not having it in my hand.

It wasn't the only part of me I couldn't bear at the moment.

Otto took my arm and helped me out of the house, back across the street to the car. He was a bloody mess; I didn't know how he was walking, let alone lending me support.

He closed the car door behind me and walked around to get

behind the steering wheel. His hand paused over the ignition uncertainly for a moment.

"What you did," Otto said, not looking at me. "What you just became in there..." But words failed him.

"That," I said, swallowing back a sob before pressing on. "That is the reason that Edward belongs with Ivy."

And then there was no stopping the tears.

CHAPTER 20

Otto drove me back to the charm school and helped me up the steps to the front door where an anxious Brianna and Sophie were waiting.

"What happened?" Brianna asked as she put an arm around me and guided me towards the parlor.

"Otto!" Sophie cried. "You're bleeding. Everywhere."

"Yeah," Otto said, already turning back towards his car.

"Wait!" Sophie said. "You need medical attention."

"I'll get it," he said. "Take care of Amanda. But get back home first."

"Home?" Sophie repeated.

"Just now, you'll all be a lot safer in 2018."

"2018?" Sophie said, even more confused.

"Crap, Otto," I said, pulling away from Brianna to go back to the door. "Evanora."

"I don't know who she is," he said.

"If you see her again, run," I said.

Otto gave a humorless laugh. "The best advice for all witches, right?"

"If you need us," Brianna said, "come back here and leave us a note. We'll get it."

"But wait," I said. "Won't he be able to see the students, and them him, if we aren't here to trigger the protective spells?"

Otto threw his hands up in the air. "I've had all I can take for one night. I'll be just fine. You three need to get gone."

"Otto," I said, detaining him again. "Thank you. For everything."

"Don't make it sound so final," he said. "We'll talk again."

Then he got into his car and drove away.

"You have a lot of explaining to do," Sophie said with a stern frown. "Do you have any idea how worried we were when you never came back?"

"And with good reason, apparently," Brianna said, examining my neck. Her probing fingertips were finding every tender spot.

"We do have to get out of here," I said. "I have a lot to tell you, but not here."

They both frowned at me but didn't argue.

Five minutes later, we were back in the charm school kitchen with all the shiny modern appliances. Sophie filled the kettle to make us tea.

"I can put some salve on that," Brianna said, once more examining my neck.

"Later," I said. "I barely feel it when you're not touching it."

"It looks like someone tried to hang you," Sophie said.

"Close. Strangle me," I amended.

"How did all this with the wardrobe get so far out of hand? You were just going to ask a few people if they recognized the man in the photo," Brianna said.

"He was a gangster," I said. "Murdered by another gangster. Then there were other gangsters. And Henchmen."

"This is why we don't solve crimes that don't have anything to do with us," Sophie said with a sigh. "You didn't need this kind of trouble."

"Did you change anything historical?" Brianna asked.

"Who knows?" I said. "I tried not to. I didn't let Otto kill anyone." I swallowed hard, not wanting to tell them just how close I had gotten to killing someone myself.

"What is it?" Sophie asked, putting her hand on mine. "Did Juno find you again?"

"No," I said, staring down into the steam rising from the tea in front of me. "I don't need Juno whispering in my ear to almost reach for power no one should wield."

"What happened?" Sophie asked.

"I don't know where I drew the power from, but I had so much of it I could do anything. I could have killed all those gangsters with my mind. I could see the threads that formed their bodies, minds, and souls. I could have undone them like unraveling a bit of knitting."

"But you didn't," Brianna said.

"But I wanted to," I said. I realized my hands were in fists, even the one still under Sophie's gentle touch.

"But you didn't," Sophie said.

"I thought that temptation came from Juno, but it's from inside me," I said.

"Juno was exploiting that about you," Sophie said.

"It's good to know that, actually," Brianna said with barely checked excitement. "We can work on some exercises to help you resist it."

"Somehow, I don't think that's going to work," I said miserably.

"Why not?" Brianna asked, curious, not defensive.

"I've never felt anger like that," I said. "I was helpless. Otto was helpless. They were going to kill us both. Otto was... well, you saw him."

"Anyone would be angry," Sophie said. "You were scared. They were making you feel that way on purpose. Of course, you were angry."

"Angry might be too small a word," I said. "I actually saw red. It was like having a demon inside me. I could feel its heat inside my whole chest, and it was squeezing my heart, and I was just so angry." I realized I was starting to raise my voice and forced myself to take a breath.

"Good, just breathe," Sophie said. "You've got this."

"This isn't the same sort of anger," I said, unfisting my hands.

"No, I think you're right," Brianna said. "What you describe, maybe it's not just a metaphor. Maybe there is something else going on with you."

"How can you tell?" I asked.

Brianna's eyes lit up, and I knew she was about to list off a thousand different examinations she could perform, or experiments we could try together.

But before she could, we were interrupted by a knock at the back door. We all nearly jumped out of our skins. It was far after midnight, and even if the windless night hadn't been deathly silent, that would have been a very loud banging.

"I'll look," Sophie said, getting up from the table and pulling her wand out. She kept it mostly hidden behind her back as she stepped into the solarium.

She came back in a second later with Nick behind her.

"Sorry," he said. "I thought you might all be upstairs and wouldn't hear a soft knock."

"That's why the front door has a bell," Sophie said. Then she exchanged a little nod with Brianna. "We'll be in the library," she said as Brianna got up from the table, taking her cup and saucer with her.

Nick looked like he had been about to say something, but was distracted before the first syllable by the sight of my throat. All the color drained from his face.

"Is it that bad?" I asked, trying to catch my reflection in the darkened kitchen window beside me. "Brianna has a salve—"

"What happened?" he demanded.

"The man in the wardrobe was a gangster killed by other gangsters," I said. "They didn't appreciate me snooping into it. But it's all taken care of now."

"Is it?" he asked with deep skepticism.

"Yes," I said. "I think so. I haven't actually checked; I just got home." He was glowering at me steadily, but he wasn't saying a word. "What happened here?" I asked.

"The body disappeared," he said.

"Oh dear, that's awkward," I said. But those eyes drilling into me were relentless. "You don't think I took it?"

"I don't know what to think," he said. "I have no clue what is even going on here. I think, I really think, that I might be going insane."

"You're not going insane," I said, but he didn't appreciate my tone of gentle humor.

"Aren't I? Because no one else in the station even remembers that there was a body," he said.

"What?"

"At first I thought it was a joke. The medical examiner was having a little fun at my expense. But then Nelson didn't know what I was talking about either. And Nelson has no sense of humor at all."

"How could a body just disappear?" I asked.

"There is no record of it ever being logged in," Nick said. "I checked. The wardrobe either. And there's no case file for a body being found in that condo. Do you know what it would take to disappear all of that? What the consequences would be?"

"It wasn't me," I said. "Nick, you know me. I wouldn't do that."

"Then who did?" he demanded. "Who else knew about it?"

"Wait, so the wardrobe is gone too?" I asked.

"Um, Amanda," Sophie said gently from where she and Brianna were standing in the doorway. "We know where the wardrobe is."

"Since when?" I asked.

"Since we just went upstairs and found it in the library."

"What?" I asked.

"You stole evidence?" Nick asked.

"No," Brianna said. "It wasn't there when I left that room an hour ago."

"Amanda," Sophie said. "This means someone got into the house while we were gone."

"That's supposed to be impossible," Brianna added.

"Because of magic?" Nick asked. "A time portal thing?"

"Amanda!" Sophie gasped, as if shocked. "What have you been telling him?"

"Everything," I said. "I can't do this secrets thing. Sorry."

"And who have you told?" Sophie demanded.

"Who am I going to tell?" Nick said, throwing up his hands. "No one would believe me. I'm the crazy guy always asking the insane questions!"

"Actually," I said, unable to stop the words from coming out of me, "if they don't remember the body, they probably don't remember the questions."

"That's not the point," Nick snapped.

"What is the point?" Sophie asked with a dangerous calm. Her arms were folded with no wand in sight, but she was looking at Nick with real menace.

"That's the point," Nick said, pointing at my throat. "You all are meddling in things that are going to get you hurt."

"That's our business," Sophie said.

"That's our calling, actually," Brianna said.

"Is it?" Nick said, looking at me.

I really wished Sophie and Brianna would go back upstairs. This conversation was hard enough.

"It got out of hand this time," I said. "You're right; what I was snooping into wasn't our area. I've learned my lesson."

"I've learned my lesson too," Nick said. He sounded so weary, even more than I felt. And ineffably sad.

Sophie caught Brianna's sleeve and guided her away from the kitchen.

"It's for the best," I said. "I understand."

"What do you understand?" Nick asked. "I don't understand anything."

"You can't be with me," I said. "You have a career to focus on, and I keep messing that up. And I can't be with you. It's too dangerous for you."

"That's not what I was going to say," Nick said.

"Well, I said it then," I said. I felt hollow on the inside, like my sad little heartbeat was echoing in some vast cavern, never to be heard by others.

"Is this calling of yours supposed to be dangerous?" he asked. "I mean, isn't there some safer way for you to do it? One that doesn't involve so many one-on-one confrontations with evil?"

"I don't know," I said. "I don't think so."

"No work-life balance?"

"Not for me," I said.

"So you'll always be alone?"

"Of course not," I said. "There are three of us."

"You know what I meant," Nick said. As his anger had diminished, he had drifted closer and closer to me. I didn't look up, but I could feel the warmth of his hand on the back of my chair, not quite touching me. "I had your back before. I promised I always will, didn't I?"

"Did you?"

"Maybe that bit was just in my head," he admitted. "But I meant it."

"I can't do this," I said.

"I still want to be with you," he said. "I want to face danger with you. I mean, it would be nice if I understood it all more. I don't want to be blind-sided all the time. But surely we can work something out?"

"No," I said. "You don't understand."

"What don't I understand?" he asked with a sigh.

"The danger I have to protect you from is me," I said.

He stood dumbstruck for a moment. Then he gave a final, oh so final, nod to his head and went out the way he had come in.

I wanted to drop my head down to the table and cry, but I didn't get the chance.

"I'm sorry, Amanda," Sophie said.

"I'll be okay," I said.

"I know you will," she said softly. "But right now, Brianna and I really need you upstairs."

That was right. That damned wardrobe still had to be dealt with.

CHAPTER 21

"Do you know how it got here?" I asked as I walked with Sophie up the stairs.

"Not how, not exactly," Sophie said. "Brianna is going ballistic about that. But we know who. Or at least you do."

"I do?" I repeated. I might be too tired for this. It had been a long, long day.

"Here," Brianna said, rushing up to me the moment we were in the library. He put a slip of paper in my hands. I looked past her at the wardrobe standing right in the middle of the open space at the front of the library, in front of the doors to the porch.

It looked perfectly ordinary, just as before. The idea of blinking into the web world to examine it made every weary bone in my body cry out against it and I let it go.

There was always tomorrow.

I unfolded the slip of paper. The stock felt familiar, and I half expected to see the words "Je suis désolé" again. But the writing was different, more loopy, less refined.

"Fixed it for you. Love, Evanora," I read out loud.

"Who's Evanora?" Brianna asked.

"A witch I ran into in 1927," I said. "She was with Tommy. He was supposed to turn me over to her employer after he was done interrogating me and Otto. I'm not sure he ever intended to."

"And who was her employer? Another gangster?"

"I don't know. I don't think so," I said. Then I looked right at Brianna. "She took my wand from me. She touched it with her hands."

"Your wand!" she cried.

"You lost it?" Sophie asked.

"No, I still have it," I said, patting the place on my coat where I could feel its length. "But it's not the same. I don't know if it ever will be."

"We can make it better," Brianna said. "Not the same, but not as bad as it is now. It's bad?"

"I can't stand to touch it," I said, and my vision started to blur.

"What did she fix for you?" Sophie asked. "Does she mean the wardrobe?"

"No," I said, and fished through my pockets until I found the other note. "The sisters kept their respective wardrobes, hoping to hear from each other, I think. But the time spell was unstable. When I found the wardrobe in 1927, it was empty, but I closed the doors and reopened them, and that was there. Whichever sister sent it, I don't think it was ever received."

"How sad," Brianna said. "I suppose burning the other wardrobe made the spell even more unstable."

"Maybe," I said.

"Do you know what she did mean by 'fix' then?" Sophie persisted.

I wanted to rub some of the tension out of the back of my neck, but the merest touch had me hissing with pain, and I had to desist. "I think I do. Nick said the body was gone, the one from the wardrobe. And there is no sign he ever existed here. The records are gone from the police station, and no one remembers seeing him but Nick."

"Do you know what kind of spellwork would be required for that sort of spell? To make so many people forget?" Brianna asked.

"I imagine it's a lot," I said.

"But she didn't touch Nick," Sophie said. "That's deliberate."

"I know," I said. "I won't be seeing Nick anymore. Hopefully, I can keep him out of this. Whatever this is."

"What do you think this is?" Sophie asked.

"She's calling me out," I said.

"What did you do to piss her off?" Sophie asked.

"Nothing. She was gone long before I lost control," I said. "But when we met, it was like she already knew me. And she wasn't surprised to see me."

"Did she look familiar to you?"

"No. I'm not even sure I would recognize her again if I saw her now. I think she had some sort of glamor. I remember at the time I could look past it and see her, but I was sure the men with us couldn't. And now the details are gone from my mind as well."

"She seems proficient at forgetting magic," Sophie said.

"We should keep track of this," Brianna said, rushing to the shelf where she kept stacks of empty notebooks. She pulled one down and took it to her table to start scribbling in it.

"If there were witches running around St. Paul in 1927 with that kind of power, Miss Zenobia would have known about it," Sophie said. "I would have thought she would have stopped it."

"Maybe she's no more from 1927 than we are," I said.

"Oh dear," Brianna said. "That complicates things." She turned to a different page in her journal and made a notation there.

"So she fixed people's memories, but not the wardrobe," Sophie said. "Not a time witch?"

"Probably not," I said. "I didn't look at her in the web world. She left in a hurry."

"To see her employer," Sophie said. "Who could be anybody. Another witch. Maybe one with time powers. Maybe Juno herself."

"I doubt that," I said. "I've tried calling to Juno several times, and she's not answering me."

"Why were you calling out to Juno?" Brianna asked.

"To see if she would answer," I said simply. "She didn't. She's lying low."

"Or she's gathering others with more freedom, if less power,"

Sophie said. "If she forms a coven of her own and challenges us, we might lose control of the bridge."

"Juno is the bridge," I said.

"Exactly," Sophie said.

"They want to free her?" Brianna asked. Sophie nodded. "But what happens if they succeed? The bridge will just be gone, or what?"

"We need to start researching that," I said. "And checking the school archives for any hint of other witches roaming the area in 1927 and what their agenda might be."

"If they aren't from 1927, the school won't know," Brianna said. "The protective spell will work for them the same as it does for us. They'll just see an empty building, and the students in the building won't see them at all."

"Why did she take the body?" Sophie pondered. "Why wipe the memories? What does she gain?"

"It gets me out of potential legal trouble?" I speculated. "Unless she's being sarcastic with the 'love' bit, she thinks she's doing me a favor."

"That makes sense, actually," Brianna said. "Juno must still want to recruit you. To get you on her side, she'll be sure to keep looking out for you."

"And separating you from Nick," Sophie added grimly. "She wants you isolated."

"But she isn't," Brianna said. "She has us."

"I'm not talking about that," Sophie said. "I'm talking about the more complicated Nick emotions."

"I don't have time for those," I said, a bit more fiercely than I had intended. "None of us do, right? We have a job to focus on here, and I've been lacking focus. That changes."

Brianna gave me an encouraging smile, then added more notes to her journal.

"Maybe it's not that," Sophie said, her voice low so Brianna wouldn't hear. "I appreciate what you're saying, and as far as emotional entanglements and our calling goes, I totally agree. Short-term, anyway, we need focus."

I nodded and was about to admit that I knew she had left someone of her own behind, but there was something else going on in her eyes, some other thought.

"I'm just worried the reason she wants to separate you from Nick is that in some way we don't understand yet, we're going to need him. Maybe Juno doesn't want him on our team."

"If it seems like that's true later, I'll bring Nick back in," I said. "But for now, it's just us three."

"And that's good enough for me," Sophie said.

"Us three, plus Mr. Trevor," Brianna piped up. "I know it's after midnight, but I could really use some brain fuel."

"Did someone say my name?" Mr. Trevor asked as he came into the library wearing a belted robe over his pajamas and slippers on his feet but bearing a tray of tea, cookies, dried fruit, and nuts. "I do believe some of this might be brain fuel," he added.

"It's perfection," Brianna said, helping herself to some of the tea. "You say you're not magical, but I swear you're psychic."

"Are you psychic, Mr. Trevor?" Sophie asked before biting into a cookie.

"As interesting as that would be, I don't think the three of you realize how loud you talk when you're excited about something. And my room is just beyond that wall."

"Sorry," we all said at once.

"No need," he said, waving off the apology. "If you're awake, then there is work to be done. And if there's work to be done, it's my job to, er, fuel it. Have a productive night, ladies."

"Good night, Mr. Trevor," we all said.

"Divide and conquer," Brianna said, consulting her notes. "I'll look into what kind of witch could slip in here without us knowing and find us some better wards to keep it from happening again. Sophie, you hit the archive journals. Start in 1927 and look for active witches then, but once you're finished with that, just start at the beginning and search them all for any mention of the name Evanora."

"And me?" I asked.

"I'm afraid for you it's the same as always," Brianna said with a regretful smile. "We need to understand time magic. For the sake of maintaining the bridge, we need to know all we can. But you're really the only one who can tackle that."

"I'm on it," I said, and took a handful of smoked almonds before going back to my little alcove of books. The book Brianna had wanted me to start with was still there on the top of the pile, waiting for me.

I scooped it up as well as my own journal and brought them to the far side of the library to curl up in one of the window seats.

It was still darkest night beyond the glass, but in a few hours, it would be dawn. And I just knew I would still be awake to see it.

I was just settling in with a blanket tucked around my legs when something caught the corner of my eye, something fluttering out in the night. All of my nerves rang loudly in red alert, and my hand started inching towards my wand.

But it was just snow. I laughed to myself and forced myself to relax. I was getting pretty jumpy if the sight of a few flakes was enough to have me ready to try flinging spells.

I let the book wait for a few minutes more, watching the sparse flakes grow in size and number as they danced under the streetlight below.

Winter was finally starting, and it looked like it was going to be just as magical as anything we three witches could conjure. I watched the glittering drifts join together to form a proper blanket of snow, until the last bit of ugly bare ground was covered in sparkling flakes. Then I turned my mind back to my book.

This time in the wrestling match between me and this book, I was going to be the victor.

CHECK OUT BOOK FOUR!

The Witches Three will return in Old World Charm, out now!

When nothing and no one holds you to the present, why not celebrate the new year 91 years ago?

So think Amanda Clarke and the rest of the Witches Three. They head back in time to ring in 1928, drinking bootleg champagne with the wealthiest members of St. Paul society, honest businessmen and gangsters and those who dwell where those categories overlap.

But when a surprise wedding engagement announcement becomes an even more surprising murder of the bride-to-be, the Witches Three find themselves wrapped up in yet another mystery.

Because even if it's not your time era, when the chief suspect is your close friend, you don't opt out. Or so says Amanda Clarke.

Old World Charm, Book 4 in the Witches Three Cozy Mystery Series!

THE VIKING WITCH COZY MYSTERIES

In case you missed it, check out Body at the Crossroads, the first book in the Viking Witch Cozy Mystery Series!

When her mother dies after a long illness, Ingrid Torfa must sell the family home to cover the medical bills. Her career as a book illustrator not yet exactly launched, Ingrid faces two options: live in her battered old Volkswagen, or go back to her mother's small town in northern Minnesota.

The small town that still haunts her dreams more than a decade since she last visited it. Or rather, not the town but the grandmother.

All of the drawings she fills notebooks with witches and the trolls that do their bidding? Not as whimsical in her nightmares as she sketches them in the bright light of day.

If not for her beloved cat Mjolner, living in the Volkswagen just might tempt her.

But the cat wants four walls and a door, so north she goes. And finds trouble in the form of a dead body before she even finds her grandmother's little town. How much can a town of stoic fishermen possibly be hiding?

As Ingrid is about to find out, quite a lot.

Body at the Crossroads, the first book in the Viking Witch Cozy Mystery Series!

THE WEAL & WOE BOOKSHOP WITCH MYSTERIES

In case you missed it, check out The Teashop Terror, the first book in the new Weal & Woe Bookshop Witch Mystery Series!

No one knows more about every branch of magic than Tabitha Greene. She devoted years to studying the most esoteric texts, hunting down the most obscure source materials, and deciphering the most cryptic ancient scrolls. But her career in academia hits a dead end when no wizard will take her on as an apprentice.

Just because, despite being descended from two long and prestigious lines of witches, her attempts to actually perform any magic always fail. Often spectacularly.

But no more college means no more dorm life. And no magical skills means no real job skills, at least, not in the witchy world. And a life spent moving from school to school every few months was a life without real friendships. She finds herself alone with nowhere to go.

Then an uncle she barely remembers offers her a summer job, running his bookstore over the summer. The Weal and Woe Bookstore, located in a magical pocket world within a block of buildings just north of the old Mill District of Minneapolis, Minnesota.

Not exactly the pinnacle of all her hopes and dreams. But it's just for one summer, right?

Or so Tabitha tells herself. But unbeknownst to her, the Weal and Woe Bookstore is about to change her life.

The Teashop Terror, the first book in the new Weal & Woe Bookshop Witch Mystery Series!

ALSO FROM RATATOSKR PRESS

The Ritchie and Fitz Sci-Fi Murder Mysteries starts with Murder on the Intergalactic Railway.

For Murdina Ritchie, acceptance at the Oymyakon Foreign Service Academy means one last chance at her dream of becoming a diplomat for the Union of Free Worlds. For Shackleton Fitz IV, it represents his last chance not to fail out of military service entirely.

Strange that fate should throw them together now, among the last group of students admitted after the start of the semester. They had once shared the strongest of friendships. But that all ended a long time ago.

But when an insufferable but politically important woman turns up murdered, the two agree to put their differences aside and work together to solve the case.

Because the murderer might strike again. But more importantly, solving a murder would just have to impress the dour colonel who clearly thinks neither of them belong at his academy.

Murder on the Intergalactic Railway, the first book in the Ritchie and Fitz Sci-Fi Murder Mysteries, available everywhere books are sold.

FREE EBOOK!

Like exclusive, free content?

If you'd like to receive "A Collection of Witchy Prequels", a free collection of short story prequels to the Witches Three Cozy Mystery and Viking Witch Cozy Mystery series, as well as other free stories throughout the year, go to my website CateMartin.com to subscribe to my newsletter! This eBook is exclusively for newsletter subscribers and will never be sold in stores. Check it out!

ABOUT THE AUTHOR

Cate Martin has written stories which have appeared in *Mystery, Crime and Mayhem* quarterly magazine as well as in the annual *Holiday Spectacular* Advent calendar of Christmas stories. She is also the author of three witch mystery series: *The Witches Three Cozy Mysteries*, and *The Viking Witch Cozy Mysteries* and *The Weal and Woe Bookshop Witch Mysteries*. She currently lives in Minneapolis, Minnesota. You can learn more about her work at CateMartin.com.

ALSO BY CATE MARTIN

The Witches Three Cozy Mystery Series

Charm School

Work Like a Charm

Third Time is a Charm

Old World Charm

Charm his Pants Off

Charm Offensive

The Witches Three Cozy Mysteries Books 1-3

The Witches Three Cozy Mysteries Books 4-6

The Viking Witch Cozy Mystery Series

Body at the Crossroads

Death Under the Bridge

Murder on the Lake

Killing in the Village Commons

Bloodshed in the Forest

Corpse in the Mead Hall

Slaying on the Lake Shore

Bones by the Forest Road

Sacrifice Behind the Falls

Body Under the Café

Assassination in the Glade

Bewitchment After the Storm (available July 9, 2024 direct from me or August 13, 2024 in stores everywhere)

The Viking Witch Cozy Mysteries Books 1-3

The Viking Witch Cozy Mysteries Books 4-6

The Weal & Woe Bookshop Witch Mystery Series

The Teashop Terror

The Salon & Spa Scandal

The Bookseller Blunder

The Entrepreneur Enigma

The Novelty Shop Nightmare (available August 13, 2024 direct from me or September 10, 2024 in stores everywhere)

The Courtyard Conundrum (available December 10, 2024 direct from me or January 14, 2025 in stores everywhere)